JACOB'S
Eclipse

SHARK'S EDGE: BOOK ELEVEN

VICTORIA BLUE

JACOB'S
Eclipse

SHARK'S EDGE: BOOK ELEVEN

VICTORIA BLUE

WATERHOUSE PRESS

For David—with all my heart.

CHAPTER ONE

PIA

"Jacob, what are you saying? Who took Vela home?" I was yelling into the phone when Grant threw open his passenger side door and was to me in seconds. He wrapped his arms around me and held me against his tall, strong frame.

"The man said he was her uncle Caleb."

I pushed out of Grant's embrace, panic lending me physical strength I didn't normally possess. "That can't be . . . no . . . Jake, no. They must have made a mistake! My brother Caleb died at birth with our mother. What the hell is going on? Where is our daughter?"

"She's missing, Cass."

Thank God Grant stayed close and immediately supported my body. Otherwise, I would've crumpled to a heap right there in the parking lot. He guided my collapsing figure into the vehicle and slid in beside me. I had a staticky awareness of someone else in the car with us, and the two were speaking in clipped, rushed sentences. My brain was shutting down to basic functions, though, and I couldn't make sense of their conversation.

I couldn't make sense of anything.

Terribly confused, I asked Grant, "What's going on? What happened?" With every question I asked, two more sprouted in my mind. "Where are you taking me? Grant?" My head swam with a miasma of thought fragments. None lining up to make one solid idea I could make use of.

"Pia, sweetheart, try to calm down. I know that's easier said than done right now," my tall friend said.

"I'm so confused. I need to check my sugar, I think," I mumbled while rubbing my forehead. Rummaging through my purse, I remembered, just like when I looked for my kit while at the hospital, I had moved it to my briefcase. My briefcase was in my car—in the parking lot we just peeled out of.

Wait... the hospital.

"Grant! Where are we going?" Just like that, the panic was back in full force. "Wren is back there in that emergency room. Alone!" My head spun like I was on the Mad Tea Party ride at Disney. I hated that damn ride every time I was on it.

"My testing supplies are in my briefcase in my car," I explained while thumbing over my shoulder. "Back there at the hospital. We have to double back. And for the last time, Grant Twombley, where the hell are you taking me?" I asked at a volume much louder than appropriate for inside a car.

Immediately after that outburst, my mind careened out of control, and I had to close my eyes. My neck felt like a rusty hinge when I let the weight of my whole head loll back against the leather seat.

Whose car were we in? Grant didn't drive, and Rio's car was much smaller than this one. I peered around the downward curve of the driver's seat to get a look at our escort.

It was Elijah. Okay, that made more sense. On to the *where* and *why* of my puzzle.

Grabbing his arm, I rushed out in one long breath, "Elijah, you have to make a U-turn here and go back to St. Thomas. I need my insulin and testing supplies."

"All right. On it. Please calm down, though. We're going to find her. I swear if it's the last thing I do, Pia. We will find her," my friend behind the wheel vowed while swinging the car through the intersection and heading back in the opposite direction.

Then it all came flooding back. Like spark plugs to my brain's engine, his promise reignited my mind. Adrenaline acted as the combustible fuel, and all the facts we knew started burning my imagination with made-up scenarios and horrifying images of my terrified little girl.

"No! Wait! Maybe we should just go. Go to the school. I'll get what I need from home, or Wren can get it for me," I said without thinking.

"Cassiopeia." It was Grant who called my name in a formidably dark timbre.

While I appreciated his attempt to head off my hysterics, the man was about fifteen seconds too late.

"Grant, I'm so scared. They have my baby. Someone has my child." I whimpered the last few words while tears, uninvited and unwelcomed, tracked down my cheeks in hot, persistent rivulets.

Elijah pulled alongside my vehicle, and I hurried to grab my belongings from the back. I stood up from bending to snatch something that had rolled out of my bag, and my gaze landed on Vela's booster seat.

The seat she sat in without argument because she knew the rule. The seat she sat in because her safety had always been my number-one priority. I sank to my knees on the blacktopped parking lot and fractured. I was on the opposite side from where the guys pulled in, so I wasn't sure how long I huddled there, sobbing and holding myself together with my arms banded around my midsection.

I could not lose that child. I couldn't live a day without her in it. From the moment I found out she existed, she was my everything.

"Please no, no, no. Please no, no, no." I just kept rocking back and forth, pebbles digging into my knees and probably tearing my hose, but it just didn't matter. If I didn't have my sweet, beautiful, innocent star in my sky, nothing else mattered.

Grant came from the back of the car and Elijah rounded from the front. They converged on me and lifted me to my feet. Grant bent down and took my briefcase in hand while Elijah ducked low enough to put us at equal eye level.

"Dub, listen to me. You have to hold it together right now. You are one of the strongest people I've ever known. You've seen plenty of shit in your life. I know you have it in you to pull yourself together. I need you to. Your daughter needs you to."

I was nodding along with his lecture by the end. I absorbed his supportive comments and felt his physical strength where he held me. In his eyes I saw his understanding of our joint history and of the experiences Bas and I had endured alone. Most importantly, and I believe what finally compelled me to move my feet in the direction of his idling car, was the familial love we had for each other and the knowledge that these two men would tear whoever did this limb from limb. When we found the person responsible for all this, they were as good as dead.

Car doors slammed. Seat belts buckled. Engine noises reverberated through the car. And then . . . deafening silence. I couldn't be sure any of us were even breathing, judging by the potent quiet that loomed between us.

More tears started, and I swiped my cheeks with my fingertips. However, these tears were not ones of anguish now. No, these little drops of fire were backed by rage. White-hot rage coursed through my entire body that someone had messed with my daughter and me, no doubt to settle some score with my brother.

I attempted speech, but my voice was small and hollow. "Is this . . ."

The men didn't even turn in my direction, so I cleared my throat and put an exhalation behind my words.

"Is this because of Bas?" I tossed into the air for anyone to answer. "Are these the same people who have been hassling everyone?"

Hassling? What a dumb euphemism for Grant's abduction and Hannah's near gang rape. My open palm hit my forehead with a loud smack, and finally both guys jolted in their seats and then turned to look at me.

"That was so insensitive of me, Grant. Forgive me, please. I'm not firing on all cylinders here." Hopefully, he heard the deep regret in my voice. Or at least took the weird tone of it as deep regret. I'd count either as a win.

"Pia, you don't have to apologize. I still can't say the words kidnapped or abducted without psyching myself out about it." He stretched his long arm back over the seat to give my offered one a reassuring squeeze.

Elijah spoke up then. "There's no point speculating what we're dealing with until we get to the school and hear all the facts."

I asked, "Where is Sebastian? Do you know? I think he has to be told."

"He's probably already at the Benning Academy if traffic wasn't bad," Grant answered after consulting the shiny watch on his wrist. "When Jake called the office first, thinking you'd still be there, he told Bas what was going on. We came to you, and Bas went to the school."

I started rummaging through my purse while he finished his comment and could not locate my cell phone. In a panic, I turned the whole bag upside down and let all the contents tumble out on the back seat beside me.

"Can you call Rio and see if there's any news on Wren? Please."

"You bet. Whatever you need, Pia. We're going to get through this," my friend said while already holding his phone to his ear.

I unlocked my phone and saw all the notifications making a gray wall down the entire screen. I didn't have time to scroll through them and see if any were from Jake or Bas. Instead, I stabbed the icon for the *dialed calls* log and selected my brother's name from the list.

His phone rang four or five times before his disembodied voice came over the line, instructing me to leave a message.

"Why am I going to voicemail?" I asked no one specifically. As that frustration simmered, the car slowed significantly and then completely stopped.

I knew what I would see out the windshield even before I leaned to peer through the middle of the two front seats. We were in the beginning hour of the evening commute, and true to form, the damn freeway was at a crawling pace.

"Do you think the surface streets are a better call?" Elijah asked via the rearview mirror.

"It's a toss-up." I shrugged. "I think the exit is only a few miles ahead. At least we're moving."

"I think that frontage road intersects the street you exit onto. I'm getting off," Elijah decided and simultaneously put on his indicator and looked over his right shoulder to check his blind spot.

If you wanted to make it as a driving Angelino, you had to be aggressive at times. Clearly my friend was comfortable behind the wheel, and in no time, we were off the sluggish freeway and cruising parallel to it on a frontage road.

"Good call, brother," Grant said after ending his call and offering a fist to bump to our driver. He and Elijah went through about six steps to the handshake, both grinning and giving a firm nod at its completion.

At least they found something to smile about. The air in the car was stifling, and I was grateful anxiety didn't hold me in its cruel grasp like I'd seen many of the women of this posse battle.

Patience was another trait I didn't possess much of. I wasn't as short fused as my brother, but the Shark gene pool was definitely low on the stuff. I already saw the same shortcoming in my little one too.

My little one.

I couldn't do this. I couldn't do this thing called life without her in it. She gave the word *life* real meaning the very first moment she was laid in my arms. That day I had vowed to protect her always. And now, I'd let her down.

How could this have happened? Heads were going to roll the minute I walked into that school. Well, if anyone had a head left if Sebastian had been there this whole time.

"Elijah, please, can you go faster? My baby..." My voice cracked and a sob leaked out.

"I'm trying, baby, I swear I am. Every Tom, Dick, and Harry is on the road right now. Apparently all going where we want to be going."

"Pia, listen, Rio had great news about Wren," Grant offered, and I appreciated his attempt to distract me.

"What did she say? How is she? Did they tell her about Vela? Maybe they should wait so she doesn't freak out, you know? I don't know... She'll be so upset with me when she finds out I didn't tell her right away. I wish this damn merry-go-round would stop. I just want to get off." Not wanting to look at either of the guys after all that, I dropped my face into my palms and tried to calm down.

Half turned in his seat, Grant reached me with his long arm and pulled my hand from my face. "Hey, hey, come on, kiddo. Hold it together. We're almost there, okay?"

I nodded and sniffled. Damn tears kept coming at will, and the one stray napkin in my handbag was already balled in my fist and used to capacity. Grant handed me his handkerchief, and I finally made eye contact with my kind, generous friend.

"Thank you." I sniffed again. "Both of you, thank you for everything." I dabbed my cheeks and then my nose.

"We wouldn't be anywhere else right now," Grant declared. "We will find her. And whoever's really dumb idea this was will pay."

Again, I just nodded. I didn't want to approve of more violence, but the fierce part of my spirit did. Finally, I croaked, "Tell me about Wren, please."

"Rio said she's awake and alert and doesn't seem to have anything more than some bumps and bruises. And as far as telling her what's going on here, I think maybe waiting until we actually know the facts might be the best plan. Of course, you do what you need to do. You know her better."

"I agree with Twombley," Elijah added as he finally made the turn to head up the hill into Calabasas. "If this all ends up being some sort of misunderstanding and she went home with a friend or something, there's no use getting Wren all worked up when she needs to be concentrating on herself."

About six minutes later, we were pulling into the parking lot of the Benning Academy for Early Learning. I had my seat belt unfastened and hand on the door handle before he had the car situated in a visitor's parking spot.

Three abreast, we burst through the front doors and took a hard left and beelined to the main office. Bas or Jake must have been tracking us, because Jacob appeared in the empty hallway. I broke away from the guys at a run and barreled into his arms.

I wanted to ask a hundred questions, but my voice was strangled by emotion. I buried my face in his neck and absorbed his warm strength. Holding me with one arm, Jake shook hands with Grant and Elijah when they joined us.

"Guys, I can't thank you enough for getting her here safely," my daughter's father said to the pair.

Elijah started with the questions I should've been asking. "What do we know? Have there been any updates? Are the cops here?"

Okay, so my questions would've been more along the lines of "What are we going to do?" "What will I do without her?" and "How can this be happening?" Queries that couldn't be answered reasonably, but my heart was leading the crusade at the moment, and those were its demands.

"Let's go inside, and we can all talk together. My darling," he said to me directly, "did you check your sugar? You doing okay?"

I snaked my arms around his waist and smiled up at him. It was a pithy version of the usual expression, but I felt lucky to have gotten that much out. "Yes, I took care of everything on the drive. My God, it seemed like we were going to sit in traffic all night."

He was such an incredible partner. Still thinking about me when we were in such a desperate situation.

Not depending on other people had always been a major component to my life's law and order. In that moment, however, I couldn't deny how good it felt knowing I wasn't facing this terrifying experience alone.

CHAPTER TWO

JACOB

The moment I got my arms around her, I could feel her entire body tremble. First, I checked in with her and made sure she had tested her blood sugar. In my head, that seemed like a better reason for the quaking than the actual cause.

I knew she'd be upset. God, that word seemed so inadequate for how this feeling of impotence jangled through my whole system. Honestly, I didn't feel like I could support both of us in this situation, but I would do it anyway. She would see I could be a confident guide she could follow when things were difficult. Even though our history screamed she didn't believe a word of that.

It was standing room only inside the principal's office. Pia broke away from my embrace and lunged for her brother. Most of the people in the room averted their eyes as though they were intruding on a private moment. The anguish coming from that embrace was palpable in the stuffy air, and I would have given anything to relieve her of the despair.

My woman stepped back from Sebastian and asked to no one and everyone, "Where are the authorities? How did we make it here before them?"

I wasn't sure how she'd feel about the information she was about to learn, so I reached for her hand to reassure her. Or me, maybe.

"Your brother and I agreed to not get the police involved at this time," I announced. Maybe throwing Shark under the bus to cushion my fall was cowardly, but I knew Pia trusted him with her life. It seemed like presenting a united front on the issue would be our best plan of attack.

She wasn't buying it for a second, though.

"Are you fucking insane?" she shouted, and several of the uptight administrators recoiled as though her profanity hurt them physically.

Give me a fucking break.

"Dub, calm down. Between his family's notoriety and ours, it seemed like getting those clowns involved would just slow things down," Shark explained. "You know Elijah has access to some of the best investigators in the world."

"Where are her belongings?" Elijah asked. "We're sending search dogs out into the canyons, and if they have something of hers to scent, it would be helpful."

I spoke up then. "It looked like she had her backpack on in the video footage we watched. Did she wear a jacket this morning?" I looked to her mother for the answer.

"I—I don't think she did. I can't even remember what she was wearing." After she answered, a fresh round of tears started.

Wrapping her in my arms again, I gently rubbed her back and stroked her hair. When she looked up at me through reddened eyes, my heart actually ached in my chest.

"What kind of mother am I?" she asked but didn't pause long enough for anyone to respond before she went on. "I'll tell you . . ." she whimpered as her emotions took over. "The worst kind. I may never see my child again, and I don't even know what she had on the last time I saw her."

My tone shifted to a lower resonance, and I said, "You stop talking like that right now. You are the best mother our child could possibly have. And you will see her again if I have to search every fucking house on this continent myself." I meant every word of the vow.

Then, as if jolted by an open current, she jerked from my arms. "Oh my God. How did I forget? Where did Elijah go?" She frantically swung her head left to right, and if she saw anything while making the hysterical motion, I'd be impressed.

Banks barged back into the room after someone poked their head out into the corridor to get him.

"What is it? You look like you remembered something," he stated, proving once again what a tight bond these people had. Meanwhile, I felt more and more like the interloper.

"Do you remember that tracking device you put in her backpack?" she asked excitedly. After his affirmative response, she went on. "I kept it, and at the start of this school year when she got a new bag, I put it in there. Can you still follow that?"

"Let me step out and see. It's too crowded in here, plus it's proprietary software and I don't like utilizing it around unsecured people."

Sebastian got the attention of the principal and asked over the din, "Can we cull the herd here? Most are just milling around waiting for gossip anyway."

The principal scowled at the man but followed through with effective action. After about ten minutes, the crowd in the room was reduced by at least half.

When I could get Bas's notice, I motioned him over to where his sister and I stood.

"What's up, junior?" he asked.

Now it was my turn to give him a disapproving look, but

I still asked, "We're going to move base camp to Pia's house or somewhere other than here. They aren't doing anything to help, and we have all the camera footage at this point. I think the longer we stay here in public, the more likely something will be leaked to the press."

"Solid point. You good with that? Your house as command central?" the take-charge man asked his little sister.

But Pia bristled at the thought of leaving the school. "No. What if she just wandered off and comes back here? If everyone goes home, we won't know, and then—"

"Dub, listen. She didn't wander off. We watched the security footage of her walking out to the parking lot with an unidentified person and getting in his car."

"She just got in the car?" Pia's voice rose with disbelief. She shook her head vehemently. Behind fingers pressed to lips, she stifled her cry. "She knows better than that. We talked about that."

Her desperate eyes searched mine, and all I could do was open my arms for her to step into.

I held her to my chest, and she sobbed. Bottom line: I needed to take her home. At least she'd be in the comfort of her own, familiar surroundings. If she needed to express emotions, she wouldn't have to worry who was nearby to bear witness.

"I need to get her out of here. We'll see you all over at the house." I made the call, and if they didn't like it, they didn't have to come. "I think Mama needs to eat something and maybe lie down."

"I'm not hungry," she groused. "Or tired."

"We'll see," I mumbled with my lips pressed into her hair and fixed my eyes on Shark over her head. Her familiar scent brought a moment of calm, so I wrapped my arms around her shoulders and pulled her even closer. "We'll get her back, Cass. I promise, if it's the last thing I do, we'll get her back."

The drive home was silent. Pia stared out the passenger side window, and I dug through my memory while I drove. Why would someone do this? Who did I know who harbored a grudge so intense they would endanger a young child? My instincts said this had nothing to do with me or my family and everything to do with Shark. Hell, his own best friend had been abducted by his enemies. Why stop there? But why go after our child and not his? He had a young son at home who would trigger plenty of attention if stolen. A pregnant wife, too.

There were other unthinkable possible motives for a young girl's disappearance. None of us had the balls to talk about those nightmarish reasons aloud, but everyone had to be thinking the same things I was.

At Pia's house, I pulled into the driveway and shut off the engine. "Is this okay?" I asked the back of her head. She hadn't looked anywhere but out the window the whole way home. Hadn't uttered a single word.

"Cass?" In an effort to break through her trance, I used her name. But that made no difference. Purposefully dropping my voice into the deepest range I could accomplish, I tried one last time. Honestly, she was beginning to worry me.

"Cassiopeia."

With a jerk of her face to the left, she said, "Huh? What?"

I offered my hand, palm up. A silent request for her to put herself in my care. If only for an hour … shit, I'd take twenty minutes. I needed to connect with her. I knew a lot had fallen to pieces in the span of one afternoon, but I wanted her to know she could lean on me.

"Turn toward me instead of drifting away from me."

I explained when she looked at my waiting hand and then leveled her gaze with mine. "Darling, please."

She reached over the armrest and entwined her fingers with mine. Her skin was arctic, and she was trembling.

Instantly, I let go of her hand, threw open my door, and hustled around to her side of the car. Confusion set in because of my abrupt actions, but feeling her physical state on top of viewing it brought me to a quick decision. She would be cared for whether she liked it or not. We didn't need two women in the hospital while searching for our child. If she wouldn't take proper care of her most basic needs, I'd do it for her.

I yanked her door open, slid my arm under her thighs, and lifted her into my arms. Of course, she began to protest the moment she made sense of what I had planned.

"Jacob, no. I can walk, for God's sake," she whined while I strode to the front door.

"Open the door, woman," I instructed rather than addressing her objection.

"Seriously, Jake. Put me down. What will my neighbors think?"

"If your neighbors have nothing better to do than watch out their front windows, they'll think, *Wow, that lady with the blue door is so lucky to have a man who loves her the way that guy obviously does*," I explained and felt pretty proud of myself for coming up with such a great response so quickly. It was a rare opportunity to sneak in a comment about how I felt about her disguised as a lighthearted tease.

The slightest hint of a smirk flashed across her lips, and she said, "Lady with the blue door, huh? Do you think that's how I'm known in the neighborhood?"

With an obvious scan from the ground to the very top of

the entrance, I answered, "It *is* a very blue door, darling."

Pia rested her cheek on my shoulder, and I soaked up the contact. She let out a heavy sigh that, under any other circumstance, could've been mistaken for contentment. I knew better, though—she was exhausted.

Inside the house, I dropped her bags by the door and closed the thing with my hip. Then I carried her to the living room and set her down on the sofa. I held her stare while issuing, "You don't move. I'm going to run a bath for you and then fix us something to eat. The others will be here sooner than we'd like, I'm sure."

"I don't want a bath," she said in a frustrated tone and adamantly stood to make her point. And then proceeded to weave on her shaky legs to the point I lunged toward her, prepared to catch her.

This time I wasn't as sweet. "Sit your fine ass down. Now." She plopped back down on the firm sofa cushion before I finished the dictate and cradled her head in her hands.

"Where is your kit? When's the last time you checked your numbers?" I'd bet anything her sugar was out of whack, because I'd spent four years with the woman, and these were symptoms I'd never forget. If she crashed now, it would be tomorrow morning until she felt well again.

"In my briefcase." Her meek voice came from between her spread fingers.

"And when's the last time you checked your sugar?" I demanded.

"Before the meeting," she croaked. "No, that's not right. In the car on the way to the school."

I strode back out to the front entryway where I'd deposited her purse and case. I scooped both up and brought them to her.

"Why don't you lie down? I'll wash up and get this ready."
I motioned to her bag, meaning her testing supplies.

"I can do it. What's with the mother hen bit?" she asked
while leaning to the side until her head met the throw pillow
on the next cushion over. I swept her legs up by the ankles and
laid them out fully. Then I made quick work of the gorgeous,
sexy pumps she'd worn that day, carefully setting them side by
side where they were out of the way, and then hustled down the
hall to wash up in the guest bathroom.

In college, I asked her to show me how she stuck her
finger, put the drop of blood in the small reader device, and
how to interpret the number that showed on the screen. If it
fell within a certain range, her body needed insulin to bring
the number down. If the number was too low, like I suspected
currently, she needed something to eat.

Back in her living room, I sat on the edge of the coffee
table and unzipped the little case. I carefully laid out the
supplies I would need and tried to review the process in my
head while looking at the items. I could do this. For her . . . I
could do anything.

"Finger," I said plainly, trying to sound confident.

Not happy with my bossiness at the moment, she stuck up
her middle finger.

"Very cute, darling. Is that the one you want stuck?"

She offered the middle finger on the other hand as well
and mumbled, "Pick one."

"When we aren't stepping over a big heap of shit in the
middle of the room, you're going to get it," I threatened lightly.
"You know that, right?"

"I look forward to it," she challenged with what little
energy she had left.

After loading the lancet in the device, I swabbed the tip of her finger. It took a moment of staring at the items on the table to recall what step came next, and my stubborn patient was letting me flounder.

"Test strip," I muttered and put the little piece of paper in the end of the monitor. I caught her mischievous grin in my periphery and gave her a stern look.

"Sorry," she giggled. "Sorry."

"Yes, I can tell," I replied through my own grin. Her giggle was the touch of lightness the heavy atmosphere needed.

"Ready?" I asked and held out my open palm. Trustingly, she placed her much smaller hand in mine and isolated one finger. A quick click of the lancet to the side of the tip, and a garnet droplet rose from the puncture. I dabbed the blood onto the end of the test strip and swiped the alcohol pad over the wound one last time. She'd had this process done so many times in her life, she didn't even flinch when stuck. I held off reading her number aloud because I thought she had dozed off.

Sure enough, her sugar was low. Either one of us could've predicted that without the finger poke. But getting the actual number determined just how off her body was and helped her avoid the situation becoming dangerous.

Her little journal wasn't in the kit, so I suspected these days she had something on her phone where she was recording the results. I disposed of the used supplies in their proper places and packed everything neatly away so it would be ready for her the next time she used it.

A soft sigh came from my beautiful woman, and I was positive she'd dozed off. After the day she'd had, there was no way I would wake her. Maybe in an hour I'd insist she eat something, but clearly her body needed rest. The stress of the past six hours had taken its toll.

I decided to text the guys and ask them to delay their arrival by twenty or thirty minutes so she could have an undisturbed nap.

Also, I reminded them of my number so they could message me directly with any updates and not wake Pia. Everyone understood, and several messages approving the plan came back within moments of sending the request.

That gave me a half hour to get some dinner together for Pia. In the kitchen, I shuffled things around in the refrigerator and frowned. The pickings in there weren't very promising, and I remembered she had a second one in the laundry room. Unfortunately, that one was just filled with drinks and a few odd condiments. At this rate, I'd be calling Grubhub and having something delivered. I definitely needed her input on what she wanted, though, so that had to wait too.

I really wanted to talk to my brother. Or one of my brothers. I gravitated to Law more than the others, but when we'd spoken this morning, he'd told me he had a date tonight. There was no way I'd call him in the middle of it, especially with news like this.

The fact that I hadn't had a chance to tell my family I was a father yet was the icing on this fucked-up cake. And fine... maybe I'd had plenty of opportunities to talk about it but just hadn't been ready to.

There would be so many questions to answer and comments under breaths, I hadn't mustered the courage to deal with it all. So now, Karma was bending me over to teach me a serious lesson for taking them all for granted. I really could use an ear at the moment.

We had to find her. I'd just gotten her in my life and

couldn't stand the thought of never seeing her again. With my elbows on the kitchen island, I cradled my face in my palms and choked back the sudden onslaught of emotion.

Why was the world so cruel? How could a grown man possibly want to hurt a child? From stray thoughts about my niece and what she'd endured to my own daughter now and how scared she must be. Ugly thought after horrible mental image bombarded my normally orderly mind, and I began to tremble. I wouldn't be able to contain the pain much longer. With Pia resting quietly in the other room, I gave in to the toxic thoughts pressuring my imagination and wept.

I couldn't remember the last time I cried. Well, not true. It was over the queen presently resting in the other room. I swore then that no female would ever earn my tears again. I was ashamed of falling apart the way I had when Pia left me. In the Masterson house, boys were raised to be men. And my father always preached that boys didn't cry or wear their hearts on their sleeves. No way in hell did a man.

That took some hours with my therapist to undo after having it preached like gospel my entire life. What a load of crap—that one gender can be emotional and the other cannot. We're all the same damn species, and we all felt things, not just observed them.

Once I opened my mind to the possibility of experiencing my emotions, the world seemed like a more vibrant place. While it was true that painful things seemed to hurt even deeper, good things were more intense too. Humorous things were funnier, frightening things were scarier—all because I allowed myself to process the feelings rather than stuff them down.

After making that discovery with my therapist, I was

able to understand my father on a different level than I had before. I learned from the best, after all. The man had always been accused of being heartless—a robot. Devoid of feelings. It wasn't that he didn't have emotions. That impression of the man was the biproduct of denying himself the ability to live.

The only person I ever saw him be tender with was my mother. The man adored her and treated her like she was the center of his universe. Even though he was a self-admitted workaholic, he always made time for my mother when she needed him.

It probably helped that she was a fiercely independent woman. She always seemed to have her shit together, so the occasions of her needing him were rare. But not nonexistent.

I witnessed him attend to her after each of my young siblings were born. He was as smitten with babies as she was. To hear them tell it, it was only by medical necessity that they stopped at ten.

They had to be told about Vela—and soon. If this story broke in the media and they were blindsided, I'd be even more of a black sheep than I already was. Not wanting to be involved in the family business had already secured my position as an outsider in many respects. At family gatherings, when everyone else was talking about mergers and dividends, I stood on the fringe, listening with half an ear. I just didn't have that side of my brain engaged.

Pia's stirring brought me back to the most important thing. Her. I walked back into the living room, where she was just waking up from that much-needed nap. Although it could've been longer, she needed to eat.

"Hey there," I said quietly and sat on the edge of the sofa. She turned to her side and made more room for me. Even after all she'd been through today, she looked so beautiful in her relaxed state. After brushing her hair off her forehead, I planted a chaste kiss there.

"How about something to eat?" I proposed.

She scrunched up her face, but I wouldn't stand for her letting her body plummet into a dangerous situation. I gave her my best bossy and assessing look.

"Jake," she started, but I cut her off with a firm press of my lips to hers. Instantly, she yielded to me, and her body sank deeper into the sofa. As much as I wanted to mount her right there, I had to stay focused on her health.

"No, you will eat. Our daughter needs us right now, Cass. More than ever. We have to stay strong. I can either cook something for you, although your refrigerator looks a bit sad, or I can order something in. What sounds good?"

CHAPTER THREE

PIA

"I know you're right," I admitted before his bossiness ramped up. "Nothing sounds good, though. I'll be lucky to keep it down."

"Okay, so let's go for something easy on the stomach. Soup?"

"Mmm, that sounds good, actually. I think I have some cans in the pantry. Let me up." I pushed at his hip since he had me blocked in with his dominant frame.

"No, I want you to stay lying down a bit longer. I can handle warming up soup."

"I'm guessing no one called while I was napping?" I asked hopefully.

Jake just shook his head, and a wave of sadness washed over his face. I felt like the most selfish person when I realized I hadn't once asked him how he was doing through all this.

"You doing okay? I'm so sorry. I've been so self-centered and haven't asked you that one time."

We both stood then, and he pulled me against his body, holding me there with strong arms around my shoulders. He pressed his lips to the side of my head, and I felt the warmth of his breath filter through my disheveled hair.

"Listen to me," he rumbled beside my ear. "You're the

furthest thing from self-centered a person can be," he said and then chuckled. The sound lacked any sort of humor, though, and I pulled back to see his face.

"What?" I asked.

"I was thinking how ironic you saying that is."

I wasn't following his line of thought, and the screwed-up expression on my face must have conveyed that.

"All of this started because you went to help someone. Your friend, or assistant, or nanny—I don't know, whatever you call her."

"Jacob . . . " The warning intention was clear in my voice.

Now he was the one to pull a confused face.

"Are you insinuating this is my fault? Our daughter is missing because I went to help Wren instead of picking her up at school?" Tears clouded my vision along with a red edge of anger.

He quickly scooped up both my hands in his and placed them over his heart. "No, darling, that's not what I was saying at all. The thought never crossed my mind. Don't you blame yourself either."

"I'm not," I snapped. But was I? On some level, of course I was. A mother's number-one job is to protect her young from the evils of the world. Was I too busy saving the day for Wren that I basically abandoned my child? The tears came heavy and hot, and I fell back to sit on the sofa.

Jake dropped to his knees in front of me and pulled my hands away from where they were shielding my face. I sucked in a big breath and continued to fall apart.

"I think we all know who's really at fault here, Pia. And it isn't you or me." A bitter twist to his tone made me pause long enough to focus on what he was saying.

"What? What do you mean?" Shit. I was so exhausted, I couldn't string two thoughts together, let alone decipher someone else's.

But Jacob just tilted his head to the side a bit—your basic *give me a break* expression.

"Seriously, Jacob. Spell it out. What are you talking about? Do you know something you're not telling me?" I accused, the first signs of hysteria grappling at my psyche.

"Calm down, my love," he hushed and drew me into the safety of his embrace. "You know everything I know."

"Then what are you saying? Or not saying, more like."

"I'm talking about Sebastian. It can't be that difficult to draw that conclusion, can it? Lately, his closest friends have all had traumatic brushes with someone out to get him. Given those events, why would you be spared? I'm kicking myself for not putting the pieces together sooner, honestly. You and Vela have been in danger right under my nose, and I did nothing to protect you."

"No," I replied adamantly. I looked my man in the eyes. "Now it's my turn to insist you stop that train of thought. Like you just did for me. This is no more your fault than it is mine. We're wasting valuable time and energy blaming ourselves for something that was probably as random as any other . . . " But I drifted off there. I couldn't bring myself to say it.

My child was kidnapped.

Thankfully, the doorbell dragged me back from that ledge.

"That must be everyone else. Please don't start pointing fingers. It won't do our daughter any good for us to be divided right now," I warned Jacob as he walked with me to the front door. "We all need to be on the same team."

My brother led the group inside before I could open the

door fully. His hair was unruly, likely from him running his hands through it like I'd seen him do so many times when he was stressed. Grant and Elijah followed right behind him but were involved in their own quiet conversation as they entered.

I hugged each of the guys and held on to Bas a bit longer than the others. I was so used to him fixing everything that went wrong in my life, his comforting embrace meant so much more.

"Has there been any word?" Grant asked, beating me to the punch in asking the same question of them.

Shaking my head *no*, I tried to stuff my emotions into a tidy box and cram the lid on top so I could focus on devising a plan. Tears stung the backs of my eyes, and raw emotion clogged my airway. It felt like I hadn't had a full lungful of air since I first heard the news.

Knowing me all too well, my brother asked, "You okay, Dub? Have you eaten?"

With a watery smile and a quick shake of my head, I stammered, "No, not really. Put yourself in my shoes," I muttered under my breath, "God forbid something like this ever happens again." Louder, I said, "How would you be coping?"

"Not well, I'm sure." He shook his head while looking at me. "Not nearly as well."

Jacob stood by my side during everyone's greeting but then leaned in and said, "I'm going to make that soup. You need to eat." He gave me a peck on the lips, and I watched him walk the whole way to the kitchen. I hadn't realized my fingers were pressed to my lips where his just touched until one of the guys cleared his throat and another one snickered.

Sebastian, in true form, was the one to break the spell.

"Oh, gag. Come on. Where should we set up shop?" Once a big brother, always a big brother.

While everyone booted up their laptops on my dining room table, I asked Elijah about the tracker in Vela's backpack.

"I'm still working on it, or my guys are. Let me check in with them again to see if they had any luck. My concern is the strength and reliability of a signal, if we get one at all, because of the age of the device. The power supply doesn't usually hold out this long, but any information we can pick up is better than nothing, right?" He was already poised with cell phone to ear before he finished explaining.

Jake came in the room and asked, "Do you want to eat in here or at the island?"

"Did you make enough for yourself, too?"

"That's not what I asked, darling," he replied with the start of a grin tugging up one side of his mouth.

Narrowing my eyes, I said, "Yes, I'm aware. I would like you to join me if I sit out in the kitchen, but not just to stare at me while I eat. If you aren't eating, I'll just eat in here." Hopefully he heard my unspoken admission that I didn't want to be alone at the moment.

"Come on," Jake said with one arm extended, ready to wrap around me in support while we walked to the other room. "I think I'll have a sandwich or something."

We sat in the kitchen with the chatter of my brother and his two best friends providing the background soundtrack. The rooms were far enough apart that I couldn't make out exactly what they were saying but could hear the low bass rumble of their voices.

"Can I ask you a random question?" Jacob asked.

"I'm not sure. You have a mischievous look going right

now." I motioned in a swirl in front of his face.

My comment caused a full chuckle, but my guy still waited for me to green light the inquiry.

"Go on, then," I finally said after a few sips of the soup. "This hits the spot. Thank you."

"You're very welcome. Thank you for eating something. I was hoping that wasn't going to turn into a battle."

With a raised brow I said, "What's the question?"

"Why does Sebastian call you Dub? I'm guessing it's a childhood thing, because every now and then, I hear one of the other guys say it too, but it definitely seems to be special between you and your brother."

"So observant, Mr. Cole," I teased. He waited patiently for the answer, though. I sighed and explained, "Obviously I was named for a constellation, right? My mom was a big dreamer and loved to look at the stars. In the nighttime sky, the cluster of stars that form Cassiopeia are in the shape of the letter W." I shrugged. "See? Dub? W?" Shrugged again. "I don't know. It was a nickname he came up with when we were very young. Because Grant and Elijah have been in our lives for so long, they say it occasionally as well."

"That's very special," he said. And he meant those words. Jake was like a sponge when it came to learning about our daughter and me.

He brought my hand to his lips and reverently kissed my knuckles. "Thank you for sharing that with me."

I couldn't tear my eyes away from his. We had such a deep connection when we were students, and feeling that rekindling closeness made me so happy. Every day we grew stronger. But contrasted with our daughter's abduction, I felt guilty when another emotion besides despair was on the front burner.

"We have to get her back, Jake." I whispered the thought and pressed his palm to my cheek.

He made the connection better by rounding the island and turning my stool so he could hold me in both arms. With my head against his chest, I let his strong heartbeat soothe my nerves.

"I will move heaven and earth to make it happen, Cass. I swear I will," he vowed.

Tears filled my eyes again and slid down my cheeks to wet his shirt. I pulled back to stop the spoiling of his top, and a low growl came from his throat.

"Stay. Don't rush off," he roughed out while wrapping his arms tighter around my torso. "Let me hold you."

"Your shirt . . . I'm getting makeup on it."

"The least of my concerns," he whispered and kissed my temple.

I swiped the tears away, but quickly, more replaced them. Why wasn't there more we could do? In the other room, the major consensus was we needed to wait and see what the kidnappers wanted. The men were confident we would be contacted soon. Although their words were meant to comfort, they just made me more unsettled. I could guarantee if this were Kaisan, my brother would be breaking furniture as an outlet for his despair. Telling me to sit back and relax while my baby was out there all alone—it didn't feel physically possible. All I could think about was how terrified she must be.

"I need to check on Wren. Have we heard from Abbi or Rio?" I asked, feeling guilty that I kept forgetting she was at the hospital. The first signs of a monumental headache were creeping in from the edges of my awareness.

"I'll go ask the guys. I'm sure they've talked to their wives by now," Jake suggested. He wiped my cheeks with steady thumbs while he spoke.

"Good idea," I agreed. "Let me just clean up these dishes."

"Leave them, Star. I'll get them in a bit," Jake insisted, taking my hand and leading me back to the dining room.

In the short amount of time they'd been here, the men had established a command center on my large walnut table. Elijah was on the phone when we came into the room, and Bas and Grant were listening intently to his side of the conversation. Grant looked my way and gave me a quick wink, reaching out a welcoming arm. I was taking all the hugs I could get at the moment, so I left Jake's side and stepped into the reassurance of my dear friend's embrace.

Grant planted a quick peck on the top of my head and squeezed me closer.

"Who's he talking to?" I asked quietly and threw my chin in Elijah's direction.

"It's Marc, his lead security guy on shift at the house. There's been some strange activity on his street, and they're trying to decide if we've all become overly paranoid or if there's something to it."

"All right, man, yeah, I appreciate it. I'll watch for the email and get right back to you. Thanks, Marc." After Elijah ended the call, he stood for a moment and let his eyes close.

We all stared while holding our breaths, waiting to hear what was going on. Icy fingers of fear skittered up my spine, and I shuddered in Grant's hold.

"For fuck's sake, Martha. You're scaring the mama bear," Grant snipped to his best friend.

I looked up to the tall guy with a twisted expression of confusion. "Martha?"

Grant chuckled, and I saw my brother pinch the bridge of his nose in my periphery.

"Yeah, Martha Stewart. I mean, have you tasted this guy's coffee?" Grant quipped in his version of an explanation.

Clearly this was some ribbing that went on among the boys, because everyone except Jake and me sensed this was supposed to be a moment of levity. Bas rarely laughed outright, but I saw a hint of a grin tugging at his lips.

I couldn't contain my curiosity about the seriousness of the situation at hand, though, while they razzed each other. "Elijah, what's going on? What did he say?"

"Also, before you get into that, has anyone heard from the team at the hospital?" Jake asked and then froze. I'd seen him do this before, but it usually the result was an idea for a building design and he would dash for his sketch pad before allowing any more conversation. Once, he explained to me that he had to draw the concept immediately or the vision would cloud over and he'd lose it.

"Aww, not you too," Grant said and forced a laugh.

I jumped to my man's defense. "He has an idea. Give him a minute to work through it," I instructed with a raised hand. At the same moment, I couldn't help but think what a strange time to be inspired by architecture.

"Okay, hear me out, because this is going to sound like a conspiracy theory at first." Jacob paused while everyone in the room gave some sort of signal of agreement, and then he continued. "But something about all the events of the day just clicked into a linear picture."

Sebastian was interested in what Jake was trying to get at, but per his usual demeanor, he had very little patience while my boyfriend explained. "What do you mean, Cole?" he asked in his signature bark.

"It started with Wren's car accident. Of course, it's not completely unheard of that the other driver fled the scene. But what if that was actually step one in the whole plan?"

"I'm not following you, babe," I admitted.

"You think Wren's accident was related to Vela's abduction?" Elijah asked, and my stomach turned over hearing that word. I clutched my abdomen, and a whimper bled through the cracks in my composure.

Three men raised arms to comfort me when my vocal distress hit the room. Jake was the only one I wanted in the moment, though, and they all must have sensed that. Grant and Elijah relaxed while Jacob wrapped me into a protective hug.

"This theory has merit, Cole," Sebastian admitted. "Can we get traffic camera tapes from the scene?" My brother directed that question to Elijah.

He nodded and answered, "I'll see what I can do. The city's network isn't nearly as secure as they'd like to believe it is." Elijah brightened with an idea of his own. "Once I see the footage from my home cameras, we can look for that vehicle on the streets by Wren's accident. Maybe the two are somehow related."

"We can also look at the security tapes from the school and its parking lot. If we get the same vehicle in all three locations . . . we may have our girl back," Grant added excitedly.

God, finally! A plan. Or at least a direction that seemed more like a plan to get my daughter back in my arms rather than sitting around and waiting. Waiting and doing nothing.

Clapping my hands, I asked, "How can I help?" I had to do something to keep my mind from spinning out of control. With each second that passed, I feared the chasm between hope and reality would continue to widen.

Elijah's phone chimed, and immediately he sat down in front of an open laptop and started typing.

"What's up, Banks?" Bas asked.

"Email from Marc. It will be easier to look at the recording on a laptop than my phone. Grant, you dig into the footage from the school, and Shark, you look at the accident scene as soon as I get that from my contact at Public Works."

Bas froze in the midst of waking his laptop. Clearly surprised, he asked, "You have a contact at Public Works? Shit, where was this *contact*," he sneered, "when junior here had to redesign the parking structure three times?"

"Yeah, well, it's not that kind of contact. And correct me if I'm wrong, but isn't that what you're paying junior the very big bucks for?" Elijah volleyed back, never stopping his lightning-fast typing. He also missed the scowl my brother manufactured for his benefit.

Grant interjected finally, "All right, you two. Let's focus on getting the queen home to her castle, yes?"

"Yes!" Jacob and I both answered for the guys. But that still left us with nothing productive to do, so I wandered back to the kitchen to clean up the dishes. I decided to text my sister-in-law and get an update on my assistant for myself. I didn't want to take the men off their task for one unnecessary minute.

Hey, Abbi, how is Wren doing?

Looks like she talked them into discharging her. When we told her about Vela, she nearly pulled out her own IV.

I chuckled when I read Abbigail's response because I could picture the spirited young woman doing just that. She was probably raising so much hell in the emergency room, the staff would be happy to get her on her way as soon as possible. The woman was as fiercely protective of my daughter as I was. Her vein of loyalty ran as deep as it was wide.

Jacob read the text after I turned my phone in his direction, and a big grin split his handsome face.

"You have an amazing team of friends, Cass. If anyone can find our daughter, I feel like it's these people," he said quietly. I couldn't tell if his volume had dropped from thick emotion or to afford us some privacy. Both?

"I really do. We do. All three of us," I said, matching my tone to his.

The man tugged me toward him when I offered my hand for reassurance, and I took a quiet moment to let his proximity fortify me. Inhaling greedy lungsful of his scent, I let the weight of my tired eyelids overtake my will to stay alert. My God, I was exhausted. The adrenaline spikes from both alarming events this afternoon left serious crashing side effects in their wake.

I leaned my body into his, and he wrapped his arms tighter around my shoulders. When he spoke, I smiled a little at feeling the sound vibrate directly from his chest into mine. It was a special connection I was so grateful to share again.

My cell phone rang where it was forgotten—just a few feet away on the kitchen counter. I glanced over at the thing to read the caller identification that said *Unknown Number*. I never answered unidentified calls, only to be trapped on the phone with a hard-charging telemarketer. When I snuggled back into Jacob's chest, he reached over and grabbed the device.

"Pia Shark's phone. Can I help you?" he said while I

stared at him with wide eyes. Seriously, was that a bit forward answering my personal phone that way? Lucky for him, the mini glare he caught from me was all I had the energy for at the moment. Otherwise, he would've gotten an earful.

Jacob's body stiffened beside me, and he disengaged from our embrace. "Who is this?" he demanded in that dominant tone he usually saved for me. The three men who were quietly working in the other room were standing beside us in a flash. All intense stares were on Jake as he listened to the voice on the other side of the call.

"This is Jacob Masterson. I'm the girl's father. I'll ask you again, who is this?" Whoa. Jake's voice became ice, matching the emotional temperature of his physical features. He gestured to give him something to write with, and I frantically rooted around in the kitchen junk drawer to find something suitable. I thrust a scrap of paper toward him, and Elijah produced a pen from thin air.

Jacob scrawled a note and showed it to his captive audience.

Tracing this line? the note asked.

Elijah nodded emphatically and gestured for Jake to draw out the call. He had his own cell phone in his hand then and feverishly tapped out a message to someone. In a heartbeat his phone chimed, and he got whatever answer he must have been hoping for because he gave Jake an enthusiastic thumbs-up.

"Let me speak to her. Immediately, or I'll hang up."

We all jumped back in horror. Was he crazy? We'd been waiting for this call. Why would he threaten to hang up?

"Yes, that's right. That's what I said. *Masterson.* What does that matter to you?" He pronounced his family name as though it were one hundred violent promises of its own.

He listened again, and his stare bounced from me to my brother.

"Yes, they're both here. We demand to speak to our daughter, and you'd better hope she says you haven't touched a hair on her head, motherfucker."

I tried to grab for my phone, but my brother caught me around the waist. "He's doing great, Dub," Sebastian muttered beside my ear. "Wait a second."

Through clenched teeth, I seethed, "I want to speak to her."

"Whoever it is will hang up before that happens. They want to make sure they have our undivided attention," Bas continued to explain in a whisper.

That wasn't good enough. It just wasn't good enough. I needed to hear her voice and know she was okay. Tears welled in my eyes, and panic strangled my throat. Desperation personified. I pushed at my brother's chest to get him to release me.

Jesus. When did my brother get so strong?

I couldn't budge him and considered kneeing him in the balls or biting him. I was a feral animal, knowing Vela was at the other end of that call and there being a huge possibility I would be denied hearing her voice.

Elijah scribbled a note on the flip side of the first one and showed it to my guy. Jacob stared at Elijah for a few beats and then shook his head before crumbling the paper. I couldn't begin to fathom what that was about, but Jake held that crumbled bit of paper tightly in his fist so no one else could see what Elijah suggested.

"What's going on?" I finally spat, getting royally pissed at being cut out of the loop. Were they forgetting this was my child those monsters had? My heart was pounding behind my ribs, and my patience was ready to snap.

CHAPTER FOUR

JACOB

I had no idea what the person on the other end of the call was ranting about. I tried to focus on his diatribe, but my attention was split between the nonsense he was spewing and the woman unraveling before my eyes.

Pia looked as though she was about to completely lose it. I recognized all the tells from the first night we got together in that little pie café when she verbally ran me up and down the flagpole.

Additionally, the guy was talking through some sort of voice-distortion device, so it was difficult to understand a lot of his message.

"Listen," I interrupted. "I have no idea what any of that means or has to do with my girl. Just tell me what you want in exchange for her safe return, and we'll make it happen. You have all the power here, boss."

"Don't fucking patronize me," the man sneered.

Well, I understood that charming remark clear as day.

"Oh, I wouldn't dream of it. Believe me. I'm totally at your mercy. You've made that very clear. We just want our daughter returned safely. You tell me how to make that happen," I offered again in my calmest tone. Inside, I was on the verge of my own scarring breakdown.

"I want my brother and sister to meet with me at a location I choose. They come alone. If one single person is spotted with them, my men will end the kid."

"Where and when?" I cut to the chase.

"I will contact you with that information," the mechanical voice said.

"I'll see what I can do. But I insist you release her when you confirm they are alone. I can be there and leave immediately with my daughter and take her to safety."

"You're in no position to make demands, Mr. Masterson," the garbled speaker replied.

"I understand that. But there is no reason to harm the child. You'll get whatever it is you want. Just let her go." Pleading words were on the tip of my tongue, but I did my best to keep a level head and not give this jackass more power over us than he already had.

"You'll hear from me soon," the creep bit, and the line went dead.

I pulled the phone away from my ear and looked at the display to be sure that, indeed, the conversation was done. Then I took in the four pairs of eyes fixed on me.

And really wished I hadn't.

"Is she okay? Did you talk to her? Could you hear her in the background? Oh my God, Jake, what did they say?" Pia shot question after question at me like rounds from a Tommy gun.

My first concern was with Elijah. "Did you pick up the call?"

The man was tapping away on his phone and didn't look up when I questioned him.

"Banks!" Bas barked, and that got his attention. Although

the look on his face was of complete annoyance.

"Wait a goddamn minute," Elijah growled. "I'm trying to find out."

Pia pressed into me. Tears tracked her rosy cheeks, and she looked up with so much fear in her normally steadfast gaze. "Is she okay? Did you hear her at all?"

I shook my head, and a whimper came from the woman trembling in my arms. "No," I finally choked and felt like I might vomit from the amount of adrenaline and emotion rioting through my body. "He didn't put her on. I didn't hear her in the background either. Or from what I could tell."

Grant spoke up and asked, "What do you mean 'from what you could tell'?"

"The fucker was using some sort of voice distortion device or whatever." I shrugged because what did I know about this stuff? "I guess to make his voice unrecognizable. At times it was unintelligible, so the crap he was spewing didn't make a lot of sense."

"What did he say? Try to remember the best you can," Grant encouraged.

First, I inhaled a deep breath. I didn't think I breathed through that entire phone call. "Can we sit down? I'm not feeling so great," I admitted and rubbed away the sweat that had begun to form on my brow.

I cannot pass out in front of all these other guys. I'd never hear the end of it.

Of course, thinking about it just made my head fuzzier. We all lumbered into the family room attached to the kitchen. The three friends took up the entire sofa, so Pia and I shared the oversized side chair. Having her body so close to mine was the calming element I craved. Squeezing her to my side,

I nuzzled my face into her hair and breathed her in. The grip she had on my forearm since I got off the phone turned into soothing strokes, and my anxiousness slowly ebbed.

Just as I was about to start recounting the conversation, Elijah's phone chimed again. He looked at the screen and let out a string of low-volume profanity.

"What is it?" Pia asked, getting the jump on everyone else in the room.

"Fucker was cloaked. My team is going to keep trying, but it's not looking good." He looked up from his device and met my stare to apologize. "I'm so sorry, you guys. But let's dig in here. Tell us what the asshole said, Jake."

The man was so lucky he didn't choose that moment to call me junior, because I had enough rage built up to epically lose my shit.

"He kept referring to the two of you," I pointed between Sebastian and my woman, "as his brother and sister. What the hell is that about? I didn't know you had a brother."

"We don't."

"He died."

Bas and Pia said those lines at the same time then repeated the other's comment instead. Everyone else in the room just stared at them, giving them time to come to a consensus on their answer.

"If memory serves me correctly, I think you once said your mother and brother died just after he was born?" Banks recalled with the lilt of a question, so Pia confirmed his memory.

"Yes, that's right. Our brother only lived a few hours. Our mother hemorrhaged, and they said they did all they could," Pia explained. "At least that's the information we have."

But this wasn't adding up. "How would someone else outside you two and your dead father know about this?" I presented that question to the group and looked from one individual to the next, hoping I'd get an answer.

A plausible theory at least.

But silence suffocated the room instead. Bas shot to his feet, no longer able to withstand sitting still apparently. Grant popped up next and paced in a tight figure eight behind the seated group. Elijah feverishly tapped on the screen of his phone while Pia and I clung to each other as though our lives depended on it.

I got the impression from the shit pile on the phone that our daughter's life definitely did. We needed to stay united through this horrible nightmare and bring her home safely. If we started going at each other for any reason, our energy would be divided. We needed all barrels trained on the same target.

And maybe that was all a pep talk for myself, because in the back of my mind, I was livid with the Sharks. If Sebastian acted like a civil human to the people he dealt with day in and day out, maybe the bastard wouldn't have so many enemies.

Another thought crossed my mind. Exactly what sort of shady bullshit was the man involved with? My family had more money than him and had been in the public eye for generations. Never once was a child kidnapped in the name of retribution.

"Jacob?" Pia's desperate tone shook me from my internal thoughts.

"Sorry," I said but didn't offer more than that one word.

"You okay?" Concern weighed down her tone and her expression.

Instead of addressing that question—because no, I wasn't okay. How the hell could I be okay? She didn't need to hear my fear-driven ramblings, though. She needed me to be strong and present for her. I sucked in another deep breath and said, "I'm sorry. My head is going in so many different directions at the moment. What did you ask me?"

"Can you remember anything else the person said?" Elijah said.

"What does he want?" someone else asked.

"He wants a meeting with his brother and sister. He was very adamant that you come alone. He said"—I used air quotes for the next part—"his men would end the kid if anyone came with you. I offered to leave the scene with our daughter immediately, but he didn't like me trying to name any of the terms. It seems very important to whoever this douche bag is that he be the one running the show."

Bas, being the arrogant, smug dick that he was, said, "Where and when? I'll be there with bells on. If this dipshit thinks I'm going to bow down to him, he's going to learn a quick, hard lesson."

His attitude rubbed me wrong for the last time, and I shot to my feet to get in his face. Pointing my index finger right in his grill, I shouted, "You will not do a single thing to jeopardize the safety of my child."

"Sit down, junior," Bas said calmly and pushed my hand away. "You showed up in Vela's life, what? Six weeks ago?" He scoffed at the notion. "I've been the closest thing to a father that girl has ever known, so don't evvv-er"—he dragged the word across two long syllables for emphasis—"speak to me that way again. Clear?"

Grant was between the two of us in seconds. He faced his best friend, and Pia grabbed my arm from behind me. She tried pulling me back a few steps, but I was rooted to where I stood. I wouldn't back down from the mighty Sebastian Shark.

Not now. Not ever.

"All right, all right," Grant said and shifted effortlessly into peacemaker. "Let's all take a break. Nothing good will come of us fighting among ourselves. That's exactly what they want us to do."

Whether the tall guy was right or not wasn't the point. I wanted nothing more than to flatten the self-righteous prick. After a few deep breaths, my shoulders relaxed down into their natural position, and I turned around to face my star.

Immediately, she stepped into my open arms, and we stood there for countless minutes and comforted each other. These two ladies were the only thing that mattered in my life now. It didn't matter if I'd only known about Vela for a short period of time. I was completely devoted to both of them and to keeping them safe. I would move the tallest mountain or drain the deepest sea if that's what it took. Sebastian Shark certainly wouldn't be an obstacle either.

When the emotional temperature in the room was cool again, Pia asked, "Did the guy say when he wanted this meeting to take place?"

Since I was still holding her icy fingers in my much warmer hand, I tugged her back against me. "Your hands are too cold. Do you need to check your sugar again? I know stress can mess with things."

"I will in a minute. Can you please answer my question?"

"He said he would be in touch."

"I'm scared to death. I can't even pretend to be strong right now," she confessed. "I fear the more time between when she was taken and we get her back, the less likely she won't be hurt."

In my mind, I was thinking she already *was* hurt. Our poor, innocent child was in the hands of some vengeful monster. If not physical, surely there would be psychological damage from an experience like this. Vela was almost nine years old. If she were two, we would have stood a good chance of her not remembering any of the details. But at this age, she would definitely be scarred. I had to stop that train of thought right there, or I would be sick for sure.

Without thinking first, I blurted the next question that came to mind. "If this is someone trying to settle a score with you"—I pointed at Sebastian—"why are they calling Pia's phone? Better yet, why did they abduct our child and not yours? Or your pregnant wife?" This was such bullshit. The more I thought about how fucked up this whole situation was, the more my anger flared back to life.

A menacing growl came from Shark, and I just stared at him. I was over tiptoeing around the guy. Even if he considered throwing me off his job because of my outburst, he could go right ahead. Good luck finding another architect to take on a project of that magnitude midstride. The legal problems alone would make most designers shy away from the situation. How would authorities know who to hold responsible for which portion of a structure if something were to fail? He would sit with an incomplete project for years and become the laughingstock of everyone who had an axe to grind with the man.

I'd just never paid attention to the vast number of people in that club before today.

Elijah's phone chimed again, and I wondered why the man didn't silence the damn thing. It was more active than my youngest sister's—and that was saying something. I found it annoying as hell, especially in that particularly tense moment, even though I knew he was doing nothing but helping us. My nerves were so frazzled, everything was irritating me.

"Okay, we got the house footage," he said excitedly.

Bas and I finally disengaged from our staredown and glanced over to where Elijah was clicking away on his laptop. At first, the image was impossible to make out, but once he pressed the play button and the still frame rolled into motion, it was in perfect focus. We all watched in silence as a car passed by the front of his Malibu home. The time stamp in the corner of the frame jumped ahead three minutes, and the same white car drove by again. This time coming almost to a stop right in front of the house and then driving away.

The group continued to view the recording, and the car passed by three more times over the following fifteen minutes. After one of the members of Banks's security team became a visible presence at his front door, the car didn't return.

"Can they get the plates from any of the other cameras?" Grant asked his best friend. "Shit, I can't even distinguish the make or model of the car, it's so featureless."

"Makes sense, though. If you're trying to blend in, you don't roll up in a lime-green Lambo," Sebastian quipped.

"Will you pause the shot when the driver is directly in frame and zoom in? Let's see if one of us recognizes this guy," Pia requested.

Elijah tapped away again, and the footage went in reverse and then stopped when it reached the beginning. He pressed a key or two, and we all stood transfixed by the monitor, trying to pick up any detail that might help.

The tech-savvy guy paused the video with the clearest shot through the passenger window.

"Well, definitely a man," Pia said first.

"Looks about six feet tall, judging by the top of the seat here." Grant pointed to the screen. "And the headrest looks fully extended."

"This is an old Nissan Maxima. I'd say late nineties. What do you think, Shark?" Elijah weighed in on identifying the car and double-checked with Bas, who gave one curt dip of his chin.

I guessed that was asshole for yes?

It was impossible to fathom how I would ever show this man respect again after the comment he'd made. And I didn't want to hear a single excuse about being under a lot of stress and saying things that weren't meant. I could already predict my woman would defend her brother no matter how inappropriate or hurtful his words were. But that was probably a lot of this guy's problem. No one ever held him accountable for his bullshit. So he stomped around like an irritable child, leaving a scorched path in his wake.

Well, I had no intention of turning a deaf ear to his malice. He'd shown his hand. Now I had to decide how to play mine.

In the meantime, we needed to get our daughter back, and I needed to keep my entire attention on that single goal.

Sebastian Shark could go fuck himself for all I cared.

Refocusing on the conversation, everyone was discussing the driver's ethnicity. We were all pretty sure he was a white guy with dark brown or black hair. No facial hair that could be seen, no distinguishing accessories like a hat or glasses.

Frustrated, I said, "Okay, this is great. We have a white guy in a white car. That narrows it down to half of Southern California."

"Well, we have to start somewhere," Pia replied. "I don't know about the rest of you, but I can't just sit here doing nothing and waiting for the guy to call back."

Of course, she was right. I needed to snap out of the funk I was in and keep my eye on the prize. Keep my bitter thoughts and feelings to myself. We needed to find our little star.

I pulled Pia against my side and kissed her temple. It felt like I was grounded when I had physical contact with her. For my own sanity, I tugged her in even closer. When she looked up at me with those observant deep-blue eyes, I mouthed the word *sorry* to her. I owed her more than a pissy tantrum and unhelpful negativity.

"You're fine," she muttered for my ears alone while resting her cheek against my chest.

"All right, let's look at the tapes from the school again," Grant said. "Does anyone remember seeing this car there when they viewed that footage?"

"Dub, maybe you want to go test your sugar again while we watch this one?" Pia's brother offered. It wasn't a bad idea, and it irritated me that he said it before I could get the words out. At the same time, I was so grateful my girl had these friends and family surrounding her. They knew her so well and cared for her so deeply.

"That's a good idea, Star. Want some company?" I didn't want her to feel like she was being excluded for any other reason than her own preservation. If I was honest, I didn't want to watch Vela walk away with the bastard either. I already knew an image like that would haunt me in my dreams.

Christ, why couldn't this all be a bad, bad dream?

CHAPTER FIVE

PIA

Of course he meant well, but in that particular moment, my brother's good intentions rubbed me the wrong way. After he had been so rude to Jake, I had half a mind to show him the door. I also knew he had a protective streak as large as his ego, but this wasn't the time or place for either.

Unlike my overbearing sibling, my rediscovered boyfriend was doing his best to support me however I needed—all while suffering himself. There were so many sides to this incredible man I'd never seen before, simply because we'd never been in traumatic situations together. Life while in college consisted of studying and finding time to sneak away and be alone somewhere. When a life-changing decision needed to be made, I chose to throw in the towel on what we'd built together and shouldered the burden myself.

Old habits died hard, apparently. Even now, my instincts were screaming at me to ask the group to leave and take on every task myself. That way I'd know everything was being done correctly. I was a self-admitted control freak and had made peace with what some would consider a character flaw early on in life. Doing so helped me embrace the nuances of the habit. By this age, I'd learned how to channel my domineering tendencies inward to improve myself in hopes of being the best at everything I took on. Most notably, my career and parenting. And none of that meant that I still didn't fall short at times. That admission made me chuckle to myself. *I mean, shit! Look at the cluster fuck my life was currently.*

"You know, I was just thinking," Jake said while he set all the supplies out once again.

But before he completed his thought, I interrupted him. "You don't have to do that. I'm fine to do it myself." I motioned with my raised chin toward his busy work.

He paused and answered, "I like taking care of you. Right now, especially, I'm more content to have something useful to do."

"That makes sense, but I'm feeling like a patient here, and I hate that feeling. I've had to wear those shoes more times than I care to remember. When I'm capable of doing something, I'd rather do it." I tilted my head a bit with my concluding question, "Does that make sense?"

"Of course it does. But, my perfect star, trust me when I tell you if we were going to play doctor and patient, I'd be setting up much different supplies"—he motioned to the items for testing my blood sugar with his open hand—"than what you see here."

"Hmmm. In that case, I think I'll have to schedule a check-up sometime in the near future," I replied and could hear the need in my own voice.

"I promise as far as you're concerned, the doctor is always in. No such thing as office hours for patients who need special attention," he said with a deep, sexy rumble and a naughty wink to top it all off. I shifted back and forth a bit on the sofa cushion, and his grin grew wider with my attempt at easing some of the ache his suggestion created.

What the hell are we doing?

Our daughter could already be dead, and we were sitting here flirting with each other. I gave my head a little shake to clear the lust fog and refocused on the task at hand.

We went through the procedure, and my number was right where it should be. He performed the task like an expert that time, and I got a long, slow, and thorough kiss when he was finished. For being a good patient, of course. If that was my reward, I'd let him do my testing every time. And even though I'd just internally berated myself for canoodling with the guy, it was so reassuring to feel him near. The comfort from his body heat and the safety from his size gave my head and heart a few moments of reprieve.

As Jacob was washing up, I heard the front door burst open. "Pia? Pia!" a nearly hysterical woman called. "Have you found her? Have you talked to her?"

Wren tore down the hall from the front of the house to where I had rocketed to my feet to greet her. We crashed together near the kitchen in a fierce hug. Immediately, I heard her suck in a breath and realized she was in pain.

"Oh my God, I'm so sorry. You okay? Where does it hurt? Come sit down." I shifted into caretaker mode as I often did with her. I knew she didn't always appreciate my mothering, but today... Tough shit.

I shuttled her to the sofa where I had just been perched and gently pushed her down. "Sit. Or lie down, whichever is most comfortable." I could hear the other women greeting their men in the dining room. The quiet, intimate moment Jacob and I had just shared was wildly eclipsed by the collective energy of the group who assembled.

"Would you rather get set up at your place? Maybe for this

first night you should stay here with me so I can keep an eye on you. Did you get discharge instructions? Are you hungry? I bet you're exhausted." The young woman just stared at me while I rapid-fired questions at her. I heard Jake snicker from behind me but ignored him and said, "Or maybe you want a shower?"

Wren widened her eyes and grinned. "Were you mainlining Monster again?" She patted the sofa cushion beside her. "Please come sit and tell me what's going on. Abbi and Rio didn't have a lot of details, and I think I made them crazy on the drive home peppering them with questions they didn't have answers to."

I sat down with a heavy sigh. Retelling the whole story sounded as fun as a trip to the dentist. I would never leave her in the dark, though. She cared about my child as though she were her own.

She offered me her hand, and I gripped it in mine. The action was both for comfort and to still my own trembling. Although Wren didn't feel much calmer when I clutched her fingers in mine.

My assistant fidgeted in her seat and stared at our joined hands. Finally, she leveled her gaze to mine and choked, "Pia, I'm so sorry." Tears filled her eyes before she continued. "I've been beating myself up since I heard what happened, and I wouldn't blame you if you never wanted to see my face again." She picked up the hem of her shirt and wiped where the tears streamed over her flushed cheeks.

"Why on earth would you think that?" I asked, trying to modulate my tone. I'd save the outbursts for the boys. There was no hiding the level of fear in my voice though.

She looked completely confused. My friend tried to disengage from our union, so I gripped her tighter.

"I'm so thankful you're safe and home. But why are you saying I'd never want to see this beautiful face again?" I asked and wiped more tears away with the pads of my fingers. "Do you have any idea what a major part of our lives you are?"

"I feel the same way about you and that little girl of yours. But you know that already." She pushed her hair back off her forehead, careful not to disturb the stitched gash on her scalp. Her next comment was a whimper. "This is all my fault. Everything you're suffering through right now is my fault, and I'm so sorry."

"How is this your fault? Don't be ridiculous," I scoffed.

"If I hadn't been in that accident, I would've been at pick-up like I normally am. Then Vela wouldn't have gone with a stranger."

She studied me for a moment, seeming to weigh what she wanted to say next.

"What?" I asked. Or barked—possibly. I really was trying to hold it together.

"I don't want to upset you more, but I can't stop thinking about that one fact, that she willingly got into a stranger's car. I know she's young and very outgoing, but Christ, Pia, haven't we taught her better than that?" Wren ducked her chin to her chest, as though she felt guilty for the thought.

"I thought the same thing. The guys won't let me watch the footage of it happening. But my brother said she goes with him without a single hesitation."

"And we're sure it's a dude? It could be a woman dressed like a man." Wren's face twisted and she added, "Not that it should matter if it was a woman. A stranger is a stranger. I just don't get it."

Jacob sat down in the armchair and joined our

conversation. "The guy signed her out at the front office. Just like every other unlisted person has to do." He got that look in his eyes again, as though he just thought of something vital.

"What is it?" I asked.

"I know for a fact that the last time I picked up Stella, the school had just changed the requirements and procedure for an unlisted person to pick up a student. Luckily I'm on my niece's list, but there was a dude in there that day getting hassled by the lady there—what's her name? You know the one?" He looked to me to supply the secretary's name.

"Ms. Monroe," Wren and I both said in unison.

"Yeah, her. But the man didn't have the proper credentials to sign the kid out, so she refused him. Guy was not happy, either."

"What did he do?"

"I don't know." My man shook his head thoughtfully as though the scene were playing out for him in his memory. "I got Stella out of there as quickly as possible because the guy was pissed. You could see it all over his face." He continued to explain, but I could have guessed the direction the story went next. "She is seriously traumatized by behavior like that. I didn't want an"—he made air quotes—"*incident*."

"Makes sense," Wren said quietly while nodding.

"That poor baby," I said with so much empathy for that sweet little girl. I remembered only portions of my childhood when our parents were alive. But one thing that stuck with me with exceptional clarity was how terrifying it was when my father would rage. Still, to this day, I have traces of involuntary reactions in those situations.

"But the reason I mentioned any of that was if that procedure just changed, this guy definitely did his homework,"

Jake said.

"But they don't make that sort of information public. That went out in an email blast to families," I added.

"You don't think another parent from the Benning Academy would do something like this, do you?" Jake speculated.

I shook my head the moment I caught the gist of what he'd asked. "No way. I would be shocked if that's the case. I mean, why would someone there take another child when they obviously have one enrolled in the school?"

"You never know what motivates people to do the shit they do. Our daughter also has a very prominent family name." Jake stared at me, and I shifted to defensive on the spot.

"What did you want me to name her, Jacob? That's my last name. If I had given her yours, it wouldn't have even been the right one!"

Yeah, I was pissed now.

"Pia, calm down. I wasn't insinuating a thing. You took that the wrong way," he said and started toward me.

I thrust my straight arm in his direction for him to stop. I wasn't up for snuggling now. "Are you sure you're not blaming me for this whole mess? You could sweep right in and take her away and make her hate me."

Christ, what was I even saying? Where was this nonsense stemming from?

Jacob twisted his face in confusion. Couldn't really blame him, either. I was all over the place with my thoughts. But now I had to examine these panic-laced emotions that were shredding my stomach and chest. This must've been a repressed fear I'd carried for the past nine years. From the moment I cut ties with Jacob Cole, I always worried he would find me and demand justice.

Wren interrupted my mental freakout with a theory of her own. "Well, plenty of people are experts at doing creepy things with computers. I'm sure either the school could have been hacked, or, really"—Wren shrugged—"all it would take is one parent's email account to be compromised," she finished and then cradled the back of her head and let her eyes droop closed.

"This is too much for you, young lady. I see you're in pain and you're trying to power through it. Where are your discharge papers? I want to see the restrictions you're obviously ignoring."

"Pia, no. This is what's important. Getting Vela back is the only thing that matters," she protested and sat up straighter.

"Baby, you're not going to be any good to anyone if you're back in the emergency room. Please don't be stubborn right now," I implored while stroking up and down her back. "Do you have a fever? You feel warm."

She leaned forward to prop her elbows on her knees and folded one forearm over the other. "I think it's all the commotion, that's all. I didn't have a fever when they did their discharge assessment."

Elijah and Hannah strolled into the room. The new couple was so smitten with each other and were locked in an intense eye-fuck when they appeared.

"Jesus . . . " I heard Wren mutter from beside me.

"Do I need to hose the two of you down?" Jake teased.

"What?" the lovebirds cooed at the same time.

"Jesus . . . " Wren repeated.

"You two are so in love it's sickening," I commented and quickly added, "and amazing and beautiful. I couldn't be happier for you both." Even though the timing was odd, my smile was genuine. I wanted nothing but the best for both my bonded brothers.

"Hey," Elijah said with his cocky grin in place. "I've paid my dues, don't you think?"

"Absolutely. But I'm glad you walked in here when you did. We were just talking about some computer stuff, and I wonder if it would help to share the conversation?" I looked between Jake and Wren, and they both gave some version of a shrug.

"At this point, no detail is irrelevant," Hannah answered.

When she spoke up, I was reminded that she had a near-abduction story in her early chapters of life. Maybe her perspective on this whole fiasco would be helpful. But was it wrong to ask? If she still had PTSD or any other negative response to the memory or similar conversations, I didn't want to be the one to trigger her. It was something I decided to ask Elijah the next time she wasn't glued to his side.

Jacob and Elijah dove into a nerdy conversation about computer hacking, and I leaned my head back on the sofa for a minute. I felt Wren scoot back on the cushion and mirror my pose.

"Don't make me be the oddball," Hannah pretended to whine, and I felt the cushion on the other side of me dip too. Three women...all exhausted...all for different reasons. I stretched my hands out to grope on either side until I found theirs and held on for the sake of my dwindling sanity.

After many minutes, I croaked to the still air above me, "She can't be gone." One tear slid down my cheek, having been manufactured in an instant to punctuate my declaration. "She just," I gasped, "can't."

CHAPTER SIX

JACOB

Throughout the evening, I'd kept one eye on Pia regardless of what I was doing. The churning in my gut went well beyond concern. The woman had a stubborn vein so thick and strong that I mentally shored myself for the battle that would take place when I made my next remark.

It was late, and everyone was exhausted. If we didn't recharge with some sleep, we'd all be useless in the morning. So, I put on my figurative dark hat and prepared to be the bad guy.

Rio had taken the two pregnant women home hours ago, and I heard Grant promising he wouldn't be too long behind her. Elijah seemed like a reasonable enough guy, so I didn't expect much protest from him either. Her brother was the wild card. As usual. The more I got to know this man, the more he seemed like a lost little boy. The tantrums and bully styled blustering were all the proof a person needed to witness to agree.

I made sure my motions were resolute when I closed my laptop with a *thunk* and heaved my tired body from the dining room chair. "I think we should call it a night, gang."

"No, Jake, noooo," Pia said immediately and even dragged out the vowel sound with a little-girl whine.

Sebastian looked across the table and held my stare for a few beats. I silently begged him to back me up on the call. He shifted his gaze to his sister, who sat to my left, and I swore I watched his blue eyes morph into some color much darker.

"I think that's a solid call, man," he said to me while standing. He reached his corded arm across the table and offered his hand for me to shake.

Was it an apology? I could dream, right? Maybe wiser to consider it a peace offering and leave it at that. I clasped his hand with measured strength and never broke eye contact. I appreciated what he had just done.

Grant looked at his watch and let out a low whistle. "Shit, it's way later than I thought it was. Rio's going to have my balls in a sling." For some reason, the man grinned widely after making the remark, and I figured I would be wiser to leave that comment right where it was too.

My woman didn't look happy while the posse herded toward the front door. Wren had agreed to sleep in the main house—at least for the first night. The woman had camped out in the guest room hours earlier and was out from the pain medication as soon as her head hit the pillow.

Quiet goodbyes were said with promises to touch base first thing in the morning. Judging by the daggers being tossed my way, I expected to have a stiff back by then from being exiled to the sofa.

Pia slid the lock into place and then pivoted to rest her back against the cobalt door. She stood motionless, eyes closed and head bowed until her chin met her chest. I was almost afraid to approach her.

"Star?" I said gently and then had the wind knocked from my lungs when she looked up at me. Her eyes were red rimmed and filled with unshed tears. When her chin visibly wobbled, that was the final straw for me.

Two strides toward her, and she was in my embrace. She buried her face in my shoulder and sobbed. Up to that point, each time she started to cry, she would school her emotions, and after a few tears and maybe a sniffle, she would regain her composure. This time, however, she completely fell apart. A part of me was glad to see her let it go and feel the emotions. Bottling them up would only end badly. It always did in my experience, anyway.

All I could do was hold her and comfort her through the emotional onslaught. Watching someone you love hurt to that extent was worse than your own hurt.

"All right, sssshhh," I cooed and gently swayed back and forth. "Let it out, baby."

Her body trembled as I held her and tried to infuse her with my love and strength and every ounce of positive energy I had to give. After minutes of just standing in each other's arms, she pulled back and wiped her cheeks.

Still crying, she whimpered, "How can I do this, Jake? How?"

"What? Do what?"

"How can I lie down to sleep while my baby is out there somewhere? Alone and scared and who knows? Maybe she's hurt or hungry ... or ... or cold."

I tried to pull her close again, but her sorrow had shifted to anger, and she pushed me away with considerable force.

Anger morphed into hysteria, and she bolted for the kitchen with me hot on her heels.

"What are you doing?" I called, trying to keep my voice down and not wake Wren. The girl needed even more rest than the lot of us.

"I can't sit here all night and do nothing. I'm going out to look for her," Pia said, nearly tearing the lining from her coat sleeve when she thrust her arm in haphazardly and got tangled in the fabric. "For fuck's sake!" she shouted.

"Cass, calm down." I took advantage of the war she was having with her jacket and wrapped my arms around her shoulders and stifled her flailing limbs. "Darling." I bent at the waist to get in her line of sight. "You're not going anywhere right now. I'll tie you to the chair if I have to."

"Just get out of my way," she seethed. "I can't—no, I *won't* just sit around and do nothing when she needs me, Jacob. How don't you understand that? I won't give up on her!"

"Baby, listen to me," I implored while holding her by the shoulders. "I do understand. I'd love nothing more than to comb the streets and find her. But you're not being logical."

She stopped fighting me for a few beats, but I was hesitant to release her from my hold.

"Explain," she issued, and I tilted my head in a bit of disappointment.

Not her too.

But how ridiculous were we? Like another one of his faithful sheep, she repeated her brother's mantra while I mimicked his best friend's trademark head slant. Maybe we were spending too much time with these people.

"I won't give up on her, Jacob. As I live and breathe, I will search for her until she is found," my girl vowed. I didn't miss the way her voice cracked on the last word, though, so I stayed within an arm's reach. She had rounded the bend from anger and was barreling headlong toward devastation.

When she spoke again, it was on a wail. "I cannot live in a world where Vela is not. I will not. I can't, Jake. I can't stay here and do nothing. Please," she sobbed, and the intensity of her emotions sucked what was left of her energy and strength, and she collapsed to her knees on the kitchen floor.

I followed her down and gathered her in my arms. It felt like my heart broke into a thousand pieces and floated away on my "Sssshhhh, baby. Sssshhhh." Over and over, I repeated the sentiment because the words I said weren't what mattered in that moment. I couldn't even be sure she was hearing me over her hysterics. I rocked her in my lap and held on even tighter. "Okay, Star. Okay." Peppering her hair and temple with soft kisses, I tried to comfort her. It took many long minutes sitting on the floor until she slowly calmed down.

"I will hold you all night, Cass. But you know you won't find her driving around town. She's not a runaway. She's not roaming the streets downtown."

Her voice was hoarse when she confessed, "I feel like I'm dying, Jacob. It hurts in here . . . " She thudded her sternum. "It hurts so bad I can't breathe. There has to be something we can do." Pia turned her imploring stare up to me, and it broke me all over again.

I tucked her head to my chest if only to get a reprieve from her desperation. I didn't have the fix she was searching for, and the thought of failing her slayed me. I wanted to be her hero in every crisis. But what more could I do? I despised feeling like I was disappointing her when she was relying on me to resolve this.

Every few minutes, she would shudder in my arms. I couldn't bring our daughter home tonight, but I could care for the woman in front of me.

"Come on, let's go to bed."

"Jacob—" she started to protest, but I was firm in my decision.

"No arguing. You need to at least lie down. Even if you don't sleep, you have to rest. Pia, you won't be any good to our daughter if you end up in the hospital because you exhausted yourself," I lectured while I stood and pulled her to her unsteady feet. I kissed her forehead and stared at her until she met my gaze.

"I'm so sorry," she said and broke our visual connection halfway through the apology.

With my index finger, I lifted her chin. "What on earth are you apologizing for?"

"That"—she waved her hand around trying to find a gracious way to describe her breakdown—"messy display just then."

"Don't you say that again. Do you hear me? You have every right to feel all the things you're feeling right now. I'm actually thankful you didn't continue to hold all of that"—I waved my hand around like she just had—"inside any longer."

We walked down the darkened hallway toward her bedroom, but she paused in front of Vela's door. Pia placed her hand on the panel and stood there with closed eyes. Maybe she was saying a prayer or begging the universe to bring our baby home. I didn't know. It was too intense to speak a word. After a few moments, she let her hand slide all the way down the door and then fall to her side. She slumped her shoulders and wrapped her arms around her waist and walked the last few feet to her own room.

My God, the pain of this ordeal was so profound. I wondered how we would ever go on if she didn't come back to us.

The stress of the day took us both under the moment we lay down. It was exactly what I hoped for Pia but was surprised when I woke and saw the time on the bedside clock. We'd both crashed on top of the covers, not even changing out of the clothes we'd worn all day.

In measured increments, I slid off the bed so as to not disturb my star. Her beautiful face was drawn with worry, even in her sleep. If she could get a few more hours of rest, we'd all be grateful. The woman turned into a grizzly bear when she didn't have enough sleep.

At least she used to.

Passing on the shower until Pia woke up, I crept out into the kitchen to make a cup of coffee. I nearly leaped out of my skin when I found Wren sitting at the island, lights still dark.

"Shit, you scared me," I chuckled. "You doing okay?"

"Sorry. I didn't want to wake anyone up with the lights. I'm surprised the coffee aroma didn't do the job for Pia, though."

"She was exhausted," I explained. "I'm hoping she gets a few more hours."

While I got a mug from the cupboard, Wren was lost in thought. Finally, she said, "You know, I've been thinking about this nonstop. As I'm sure everyone has been. My gut is telling me there's something right under our noses that will identify this guy. But we're missing it."

"What do you mean? Like something he said during that bullshit call?"

"No, I think it's the whole story in general. It just doesn't make sense. How many people even knew they had a brother who died at birth? I think even some of the people who were here yesterday were blindsided by that fact. And those are the closest people in their lives." She thought for a couple beats and then finished with, "That list has to be pretty damn short, don't you think?"

"I'd have to check to be sure, but I think birth records are public. Meaning anyone who had an axe to grind with either of them—Bas or Pia, I mean—could do minimal research and gather the necessary information."

Wren slumped forward to rest her elbows on the cold marble countertop. My explanation shot her theory to hell, and she looked bummed.

"Sorry. I didn't mean to suck the wind out of your sails." I gave her a soft smile over my shoulder. Holding the coffee pot aloft, I asked, "Ready for top off?"

"Yes, please," she replied and pushed her cup toward me.

"When that dude calls again, I'm going to demand he lets us speak to Vela or see her on video or something. We need some sort of assurance that she's okay before we meet any demands he makes."

"And," the woman added, "that would give all of us some peace of mind. Seeing her with our own eyes and knowing she's okay."

I gave her a warm smile. "You're absolutely correct. You really know each other well. You and Pia, I mean. I'm so thankful she has a woman friend in her life too. Not just all the guys."

"I love these people like they are my family. Actually, I love them more than my family." She winced after the second half of her comment.

I didn't let on that I knew about some of the history she had with her mother. I wouldn't betray Pia's confidence that way.

She must have felt compelled to explain such a bitter comment, though, because she held her hand up as if to interrupt me—regardless that I wasn't actually talking. "I know how that sounds, but sometime when we have nothing better to talk about or are stuck in traffic, I'll tell you about my poor excuse for a mother."

"I'd like that. Simply because I'd like to get to know you better. I know how much these two girls of mine adore you; therefore, I want to adore you as well." I smiled again, hoping that didn't sound like I was hitting on her.

"Plus, it's only fair, given how much I know about you," she teased while raising her brows a few times. Even added an exaggerated wink on the end so I knew she was messing with me. I figured there was an element of truth in there somewhere, though.

"So, she talks about me, huh?" I asked like a conspiratorial schoolboy.

"Wouldn't you like to know?" She grinned.

"I definitely would."

A new voice entered the conversation from the shadows. "Definitely would what?" Pia asked, her voice gravelly from lack of sleep.

I intercepted her before she started mainlining the joe. After a peck to the top of her head, I said, "Definitely insist you get a little more sleep. Come on, I'll lie down with you."

"I'm rested. I just need some coffee, and I'll perk up," she insisted. "Ask Wren. I sound like this every morning."

If her health wasn't as fragile as it was, I would have thought her little fibs were cute. Instead, I'd have to shift back into dominant mode and tell her what she was going to do rather than let her come up with her own plans. In true form, they never included her well-being and scarcely her best interest.

"I'll bring you a mug in bed. Please don't make me carry you in there, woman."

"You know…" The lady paused and gave me an assessing side eye. "I survived almost ten years without you around telling me what I can and can't do," she spat defiantly.

"My cue to leave," Wren mumbled and scurried out of the room so fast, the still air around us kicked up in a breeze. In a few moments, I heard the guest room door shut and the lock click into place.

"Don't get sassy, Star. You don't want a striped ass right now with so many people around to see you sit so uncomfortably," I warned while refilling my coffee. When I turned back to face Pia, she stood with her hands boldly propped on her hips.

"You wouldn't dare…" she challenged, and I really wished there was more light in the room so I could watch her get all flustered. That particular shade of pink her cheeks and neck flushed always spoke to the dark place inside me.

"Do you want to test that theory?"

Like a little angry kitty, she hissed some remark under her breath and spun to head back to her room. I surprised her when I reached out and caught her by the hood on her bathrobe and yanked her backward. My chest was against her back and shoulders, so I both heard and felt her breath woosh past her lips when we collided. It was probably better she couldn't see the grin splitting my face.

Beside her ear, I growled, "Keep it up, Cass. See what happens."

"Jacob…mmmm…" Her words ended there. Just my name and then a needy sound from low in her throat. The fact that I was already stiff and slotted perfectly in her ass crack didn't hurt my case.

I kissed her below her ear and ran my nose up and down the column of her neck several times. Her smell was intoxicating, and I sank my teeth into her flesh for a sharp bite. That spiked my cock to full attention for the first time in a day and a half.

Nudging her to walk, I steered her to her bedroom and warred with myself on the way. I wanted nothing more than to sink into her again, but I already knew she would want a shower first. Couldn't blame her there since we were both on day two of the same clothing. But, if we showered and then fucked, we'd both be wide awake afterward. Right then, I still had a chance she'd fall back to sleep. However slim that chance might be, her health was more important than my desperate dick.

She climbed into bed, pouting magnificently the whole time. I crawled in right after her and stretched out above her delicious body. With my knee, I made space for my weight to settle between her thighs, and she wrapped her arms around my waist.

"I could get used to lying like this every morning," I said in a husky tone then stole an innocent kiss.

"You always did like morning sex." She smiled up at me.

"I don't remember you complaining, either," I teased. "I don't want to kill you with coffee breath, though."

"It's totally fine." Pia held my gaze with her intense blue eyes. "Kiss me," she whispered.

"Kiss you what?"

"Now?" She let a grin spread across her lips.

"No, not what I was looking for." I fought my matching grin and gave her a stern look instead.

My perfect star slid her hands up my body and tugged me closer with her locked hands behind my neck. "Please kiss me, Jake. Take me away from this nightmare . . . even for just a while." Her voice was still soft, but her melancholy gave it depth.

There was no way I'd deny her after that comment. I wouldn't have denied her anyway. But hearing the anguish in her tone and seeing the despair in her eyes undid me.

We kissed—and kissed. Long and slow, gentle and almost shy at first. Maybe she was having the same mental struggle I was having. Was it wrong to seek solace with our bodies this way? It sure as hell didn't feel wrong. There wasn't a single thing about her beneath me that felt wrong.

As our passion burned hotter, I surged against the warm juncture of her thighs. Over and over again. If the damn clothing we still wore wasn't between us, I'd be thrusting into her harder to reach those perfect places that made her shout.

Not losing sight of the fact that Wren was just a few doors away, I reminded her to keep her voice down.

Thinking of her assistant reminded me to ask, "So your girl Friday tells me she's heard so much about me." I raised one accusing brow and swiveled my hips so my cock rubbed her pussy. "What have you been saying about me, Ms. Shark?"

She grinned between my rough kisses. "Oh, you know . . . this and tha—*at.*" Her voice pitched higher when I sneaked in a bite to the sensitive skin just below her ear.

"Did you tell her how much you missed my cock?" I taunted.

"Mmmm, no. But I definitely have, Mr. Cole," she purred.

I couldn't take the nobility role any longer. I yanked the bedding from between our bodies so I could feel her in truth.

As I untied the sash around her waist, the bathrobe fell apart into its two halves, and I realized she was bare beneath.

"Perfect," I groaned and went right for her breasts. I cupped them in my hands and lifted them toward the center, where I plunged my face. As I licked and sucked one then the other, Pia wriggled beneath me. I backed off her body to take in her expression.

I didn't recognize the face she made, so I asked, "What? What is it?"

"Nothing. It feels so good. I—I need you inside me," she whimpered.

"Patience, Star. We'll get there. Is that what you told your friend? How much you love to be fucked?"

That time she laughed, and I continued. "What? Girls don't tell each other about those things between pillow fights in their panties?" I continued to tease. "Damn, woman, you're ruining all my fantasies with one chuckle."

"Oh, that's your fantasy, is it? Let me guess... They're all dressed like naughty cheerleaders, schoolgirls, and nurses?" Her blue eyes darkened to navy with arousal.

"I do love a plaid miniskirt. Not going to lie." I rolled my eyes in mock ecstasy. Until she reached between us and fumbled with my belt. Then the pleasure spiked for real. Still, I batted her hands away.

"No, wait for it like a good girl," I reprimanded.

Through her pouted lips, she huffed a frustrated sigh. She shook her head and whined, "I don't want to wait. I'll beg for you if that's what you want."

"Hmmm," I thought aloud. "That's not a bad offer. But I think I want more than that."

"Tell me and I'll do it. I want you so bad, I'm aching right now."

I sat back on my heels for a moment and surveyed her body from head to toe, vocalizing my appreciation. "Show me where."

"Where what?"

"Show me where it hurts, baby. I'll take care of it for you. I'll take care of everything."

"You know where," Pia answered. "Please."

"Touch your pussy. Use one finger and rub your clit while I watch."

She stared at me with giant eyes while her excited breaths heaved her chest up and down, thrusting her perfect tits toward the ceiling.

"Fuck, you're so hot, Cass. Do it. The sooner you do what I ask, the sooner you'll get what you want." I moved off the bed but didn't go far. Standing at her bedside, I opened my pants and reached my hand into my boxers to relieve some of the discomfort from being jammed inside with a hard-on.

While my sexy woman watched me handle myself, she slid a tentative hand between her thighs.

My eyes were riveted to her motion, and I gripped myself tighter and groaned. "Fuck yes."

Pia made the most alluring sounds during sex. Apparently when she pleasured herself, too. A quiet whimper signaled when she hit the perfect spot, and her eyes slid closed.

"No, keep them open. Either look at me or watch what you're doing to yourself. Fuck me, girl. I feel like I'm going to explode here watching you."

Her eyes darted up and down between my face when I spoke and my hand jacking my cock. My pants and boxers were shoved carelessly down around my thighs, and I cupped and squeezed my balls with the other hand.

"Oh, shit, Jacob. Please. Please fuck me," she all but cried. "I did what you wanted. Please."

"Show me how wet you are, baby," I instructed. "Spread your legs farther so I can see."

Immediately she did what I issued. All feelings of shyness gone now.

"Jack..."

I still loved when she called me by that name. Memories of a time long ago when life wasn't complicated and delicate. And painful. So fucking painful.

That was my breaking point. Her using that name for me and seeing her arousal glistening in the low light of dawn. She welcomed me back to the spot between her thighs without hesitation, and in one sure motion, I was buried inside her cunt completely.

Paradise. It was fucking paradise in this woman. Warm and tight, her channel gripped my dick and fluttered all around me. I stilled my thrusting to enjoy the perfection of my star. I was falling apart with every squeeze and wriggle she gave me.

"Baby, I'm going to come if you keep doing that. Fuck, it feels so good." I pushed her knees back until they were against her chest. The change in position coaxed a deep moan from Pia's throat.

"Oh my God. Yes, like that. Fuck me, Jacob. Don't stop," she chanted.

"The minute you come, girl, I'm gone. Give it to me. Explode around me." Each comment was issued on a deep thrust that rocked her entire body back.

Only a few more pumps of my hips, and she closed her eyes while her mouth dropped open on a silent scream. The sight of her climaxing sent me over the cliff too, and my cock jerked and pulsed inside her.

And no, I hadn't used a condom, and no, I didn't care. Not one single bit.

I rolled off her spent body and pulled her into my chest.

We lay that way until our hearts found their normal rhythms and our breathing steadied. With my face buried in her thick chocolate waves, I drifted off to catch a little more sleep before we had to face reality again.

"Thank you, Star," I muttered into her hair. But my woman was already off to dreamland too.

CHAPTER SEVEN

PIA

I lay in Jake's warm embrace and focused on his steady breathing. My brain was running wind sprints while my body ached for the calmness only he could bring. I was the most selfish person to walk the earth, I was convinced of it. While another day broke in the distance, my child was somewhere out there. Alone. And what did I do instead of insisting we remount the search for her the moment I woke up? Indulged in carnal gratification. Toe-curling, teeth-grinding, tummy-turning gratification—true. But what kind of mother did that make me?

The kind that didn't even deserve to claim the unconditional love of her missing child, obviously.

Two versions of Cassiopeia Shark existed. For most of the time, the two halves coexisted peacefully. On the outside, the public saw one version that was successful, driven, responsible, organized. Not being conceited—the list could go on and on because I truly put effort into being the best form of me I could be. Every single day.

Unfortunately, the private, internal version of Pia Shark was almost the complete opposite. When the sun was past the horizon and those long hours stretched through darkness, I was anything but put together. I had a keen knack for ripping myself apart and swearing to any saint I could think of that I would do better when given another chance.

Growing up without a mother took its toll in that space. I lacked self-esteem and confidence that I always assumed my mother would've taught me. Being my own worst critic came much easier and seemingly more naturally than innately believing I possessed much worth. And I knew if I voiced any of those thoughts to people within my innermost circle, they'd scoff. Tell me I was being ridiculous. Little did they know, that only bolstered the negativity more.

My feelings were my feelings. No one could tell me they were wrong or right. They were mine.

"Stop," Jacob muttered into my nape.

"Hmmm?" I shifted back to the outer me. "Stop what?"

"Stop beating yourself up for what we just did."

"What are you—" I began to protest, but he cut me off.

"Cut the crap, Cass. You're forgetting how well I know you. I've been lying here feeling your entire body stiffen in increments. Bits at a time, but I know you're running yourself through the whole gamut. Just stop." He issued the whole thought without taking a breath, as if he knew if he were to leave a gap in the conversation, I would immediately fill it in with my protest.

Bastard wasn't wrong.

But I wouldn't give him that much power. At least not this early in our relationship. Well—our rekindled relationship. Walking away from what we had so many years ago changed my entire outlook on sharing my life with a partner.

I used to always daydream about getting married. My husband would be all the things a woman dreamed her man should be. Smart, kind, charming, loving, and capable. He would take care of me, provide for our family, and support me pursuing my dreams. After all, rose-colored glasses fit a girl best during that phase of her life.

Once I started experiencing the challenges of the real world, I became more skeptical. Jaded, even. Becoming dependent on another person was a surefire setup for pain. Emotionally, physically, psychologically—it didn't matter. Once a man knew how badly you needed him, he had the power to destroy you. When I started recognizing that with Jacob in the past, it terrified me.

And it was probably why I ghosted him. It took years of working with my therapist to come to that conclusion. Now it seemed so obvious. I'd had trust issues to begin with, so deep in my heart, I didn't trust Jacob enough or trust what we had cultivated between us. If I had believed we were strong enough to face the adversity of an unplanned pregnancy, I would've stayed and fought alongside him, not bolted with the belief I would be better off on my own.

Because that Jacob was a different version of the man who lay beside me currently. Of course he was. We were a decade younger, and he was immature and egocentric back in the day, and I never blamed him for those facts. He was a young man trying to find his way in life. Just like I had been.

Sebastian had beaten a few laws to live by into my subconscious mind. Not surprisingly, he harbored the same trust issues I had from our shitty childhoods. My brother swore it was the fool's bet to count on anyone but yourself. Other people always let you down. Especially when you needed them most.

"Why aren't you answering me? Did that comment make you mad?" Jacob asked gently.

I knew he wasn't looking for a fight with his initial comment. My brain loved to run off on its own destructive tangent. I'd been so lost in my own thoughts, I hadn't heard a word he'd said.

"No, I'm not mad. Sorry. I've been so stuck in my head," I admitted. "I didn't even hear you."

Witnessing Jacob in our current crisis was reminding me how unfair it was to lump him in the untrustworthy category. Now, or in the past. I never gave him the courtesy of a choice when we were expecting our daughter. I knew in my heart, and based on his proclamations, he would've been at my side the whole time if he had only known he was going to be a father.

Now that we were going through this bullshit, he was as attentive as a person could be. He was actually getting on my nerves a little bit—and that thought made me chuckle out loud.

"What's so funny?" he mumbled from behind me. His voice was deep and husky from lack of sleep, and the sound vibrated through my torso where we were pressed against each other.

"I should be thanking you, not giving you any of my bad attitude. I'm sorry about that. It's just that—"

"I'll let you make it up to me," he answered suggestively and jabbed at the ticklish spot along my ribs.

Goddammit! I had hoped he'd forgotten where the kill zone was on my side. Well, if he recalled where the spot was located, he should have remembered how badly I hated being tickled, too.

"Well look here," he teased and tried to repeat the dig again.

This time I grabbed his hand before he struck his target and wrapped his arm around me tighter. When I wiggled my ass back into his available lap, he released a sexy groan.

"No tickling," I issued and wrapped his arm around me even more. I felt so safe in this man's embrace.

"Do you have clients scheduled today?" Jacob asked while nuzzling into my hair.

With a sigh, I admitted, "I didn't even look at my calendar last night. There's no way I can go to the office today. Even if I somehow gave myself permission to work in the middle of a crisis like this, I'd never be able to concentrate once I was there."

"Yeah, same. To all of it. But I need to at least check my schedule before I have someone expecting me at their office and I'm a no-show." Jacob pulled away and lumbered out of bed. "You going to sleep a little more?" he asked hopefully.

"No, I'm getting up too. I'll call in and have my assistant deal with my schedule. I'm surprised you don't have a PA." Although I didn't make the comment as a question, I definitely hoped it would launch a new conversation. Discussing a topic other than our kid would be nice for a few minutes.

"Nah . . . " he said and moved to sit back down on my side of the bed. I made more room for him, and he took the spot at my hip. "Not busy enough. Yet." He added that last word with a wink.

"I suppose the Edge consumes most of your time, even at this phase of the construction?" That time I did phrase my comment as a question, even though I knew it did.

"That, and I've been trying to keep my schedule fluid so I can jump right on any issues that come up. Your brother can be"—he paused a moment, likely searching for diplomacy—"rather demanding. But my designs for the building were finished in the first week. I was so excited and proud to have landed the contract," he chuckled. "I spent morning, noon, and night drawing and redrawing until I felt like I got all of his wants incorporated."

"I can just imagine how long that list was," I commiserated. "But Jacob, your talent is astounding. My brother dreamed about that building for years. The fact that you translated his mental image so perfectly... It's really amazing. You should be proud of the work you've done." I watched him get more and more uncomfortable as I praised him.

"What is this?" I waved my hand in the air in front of his face. "Why do you look like you're about to leap out of your skin?" I ensured my tone was light because I didn't want him to feel like I was attacking him. Simply curious about what I was witnessing.

The normally confident man shrugged awkwardly. "I don't know. It's hard sometimes..."

"What's hard, baby? Talk to me," I urged with a soft stroke up his forearm. I loved the way his muscles danced beneath my touch.

"To hear someone sing my praises like you were just doing."

"But Jacob, you're so incredibly gifted. Surely it comes with the territory?"

"I-I guess," he stuttered.

"Hmmm," I hummed in response then went out on a limb with my follow-up question. "There's more to this, isn't there?"

"You're very perceptive, Ms. Shark," Jacob replied but wouldn't lift his eyes from his fidgeting hands in his lap.

"Well, that, and I know you pretty well, too, Mr. Cole," I said kindly and reached out to still his nervous hands.

After expelling a heavy sigh, he finally met my gaze again.

"When I was a boy, I loved drawing—not surprising, right?" He chuckled. "Every time I would finish what I thought was my greatest masterpiece yet, I'd run to show my father. Nothing meant more than that man's praise and approval." He smiled at first, but the joy quickly drained from his face.

Jake stood abruptly, no longer comfortable looking right at me while sharing this bit of history. Something about it seemed to be making him feel very vulnerable, maybe? I was totally guessing until he got to the point.

"Of course, I'd most often find him in his library, always working. I think to this day, he still takes most of his meals at that damn desk when he eats at home." My guy shook his head ruefully.

"So did he have a gallery of your drawings in his study?" I asked, trying to spur him along in telling the story. To the public's eye, the Masterson family appeared to be the all-American, Norman Rockwell version of unity.

"Oh, hell no!" Jacob scoffed. "He would find a flaw in every single one. It could be the most minor detail, but instead of overlooking a small mistake—or what he perceived as a mistake—and focusing on the concept as a whole, he would nitpick and criticize."

"Oh, sweetheart," I said while getting up and going to where he stood, gripping the back of his neck.

"Don't," he warned, but I was confused by his tone and the word itself.

"Don't what? I was going to see if I could get a hug, but—oohh kaaaay."

Instantly, his ire wilted, and he opened his arms for me to step into him. But now I hesitated because my confusion transformed to irritation, as it often did, and I decided I didn't want a hug after all.

"Forgive me, please," he said, and from his body language alone, I knew it was genuine.

But that was the thing about apologies. Just because someone issued one, and just because they were truly remorseful, the offense—or in this case, the hurt—wasn't magically erased. I wasn't one to easily accept apologies, similar to my sibling, who didn't easily issue them. I had a niggling feeling in the back of my mind that both must have something to do with our screwed-up adolescence since we both had a version of the same issue.

Another addition to the list of topics to discuss with my therapist. At this rate, I would never clear that weekly slot on my schedule for other things.

"Shower?" Mr. Cole asked with a hopeful twinkle in his eyes.

"Okay. Then we can touch base with the others and see if there's a game plan for today," I said as I shuffled around my bathroom, gathering the things I needed for a shower.

"Shouldn't we be the ones to determine the course of events? I mean, she is our child."

"Well, Elijah has way more experience in this type of thing than either one of us does. It was a natural progression for him to lead the hunt."

I watched his face screw up and then the effort he made to cover up his reaction.

"What was that? That face? Now you don't like him either?" Already, my patience was dangerously thin when it came to these men and their alpha-dog behavior.

"What do you mean *either*? Who else don't I like? Christ, that sounds like we're in junior high." My guy shook his head at the nonsense.

I didn't want to be the one to address the obvious elephant in the room yesterday, but was he going to really pretend that posturing between Bas and him didn't happen?

"Never mind. It's not what's important right now or what we should be worrying about," I said, rather than get into an argument over it.

We showered together and spent twice as much time under the water than if we had taken separate ones. There was a lot of kissing and touching, and after I gave his dick extra attention with my soapy hands, Jacob spun me around and crowded me against the slick wall. He took me from behind while holding my wrists behind my back with one hand and the other firmly over my mouth to muffle my cries of pleasure.

That dark pool of desire deep inside me that had dried up years ago was quickly refilling and swirling in all the best ways. A hunger for physical touch and the need for sexual satisfaction was alive and well just beneath the surface of every moment we shared.

When we were in college, we would spend entire weekends switching between carnal fucking and tender lovemaking. If only we had that sort of time to devote to reliving those memories. I was certain it wouldn't take much convincing on this sexy man's end either.

Out of the shower, I dressed in my walk-in closet and came out to find Jacob intently focused on his phone. He texted a reply to whatever message he had just read and finally realized I was standing there.

A slow, sexy smile spread across his lips. "You look flushed, baby. You okay?"

With a matching grin, I playfully smacked his chest. "Gee, I wonder why?"

He grabbed my hand and brought it to his lips. After a few sweet kisses to my knuckles, he said, "I need to go talk to my family. I've been wanting to tell them about you and Vela for a while, but now I have to. If they heard news like this via the media, it would be a monumental shit show. Trust me."

"All right," I said quietly. "Do you want me to come with you?"

He didn't look thrilled about the prospect of visiting his parents, and I thought if he introduced me in person, it might be easier. But that would take us both away from command central here, and I didn't want that either. Just as I was about to speak my concerns, Jacob answered my question.

"No, I think I should go alone. As much as I want them to meet you, one of us needs to stay here in case that dipshit calls again."

"Yeah," I sighed. "I was just thinking the exact same thing. Will you be okay on your own, though? How do you think they will react?"

He scrubbed a hand down his face, and that gesture spoke volumes before he even uttered a word. He was worried.

"I'm not really sure," Jake said on a heavy sigh. "My mom? She's the easy guess. That woman is the most maternal human being that ever lived." Then he chuckled before adding, "Makes sense, right? Ten kids and very vocal hopes for ten times as many grandchildren."

Slipping my arms around his waist, I said, "I can't wait to meet her. She sounds extraordinary." I watched him carefully as I spoke, and he dipped in to kiss me. But as quickly as the warm, pleasant moment formed, it was gone.

Jacob pulled away from my embrace and sat on the edge of the bed. "My dad won't be happy. Shit . . . " He gave a mirthless chuckle. "He never is. Unless he's putting someone in their place, which of course is always me if I'm nearby."

I interrupted with, "Is he disrespectful like that to your mother too?" The more I could find out about these people before I finally did meet them, the better prepared I'd be to hold my own.

"Oh, hell no. She'd have his balls in a vise if he spoke down to her. Ever."

"Well, I'm glad to hear that at least," I muttered and sat down beside him.

My man winced when he looked my way. "I'm giving a terrible impression of them, aren't I?"

"If it's the truth, then it's the truth. You don't have to sugarcoat things for my benefit. My own father was a quick-tempered drunk. How's that for a rosy picture?" I laughed, or coughed—in this case, they sounded the same. "So, what are you planning to tell them? They're going to hate me before they ever meet me."

"Pia. Shark." He stood again, enunciating each name as if it were its own sentence.

"Jacob, I know what I did to you was terrible. And unfair. And selfish," I listed.

"Star, stop. It's in the past now."

"I just don't think everyone will be as gracious as you've been. I stole years of her life from you. I know now—well, I've known for a long time—that it was the wrong thing to do."

"We were young—" he started, but I cut him off.

"Stop making excuses for me. I don't deserve them." I fumbled with the watch on my wrist just for something to do with my remorseful discomfort.

When he dropped to his knees in front of me, I shot my

gaze to meet his squarely. He nudged my knees apart and got as close to me as possible with the bed there.

"I don't want to hear any more of that berating yourself. Do you understand me?" His voice was deep and sure with the edge of kindness I'd come to expect.

For a few long moments, I didn't speak. Just stared into his soulful eyes. His love radiated from his gaze, and the exchange made me feel like no time had passed between our first encounter so many years ago and the moment we were locked in right now.

Tears unexpected and, frankly, unwelcomed filled my eyes and blurred my sight. What was this all about? I wasn't typically an emotional woman, so I could only assume the drama from the past twenty-four hours was tossing me about.

He was right there for me. Right there to catch me as I fell over the edge and into the abyss of despair. True, I had lost my shit yesterday in the hospital parking lot and again before we called it a night. But this was so different. This breakdown had nine years of loneliness, guilt, and exhaustion of single parenting behind it.

Jacob held me in his strong arms while I sobbed. Until I settled down, he comforted me in his physical nearness and his verbal adoration. All I could think was I didn't deserve this man. I didn't deserve his kindness, forgiveness, or love.

If we didn't bring our daughter back home soon, how long would it take him to realize all those things? This time he'd be the one to leave me, and I wouldn't have a thing to say about it. After the hell I'd put him through—*us* through—maybe that's what I deserved.

CHAPTER EIGHT

JACOB

"No dude, I'm telling you," my brother Lawrence said, his voice bouncing around the interior of my car while I made my way to our parents' house. "She wants me."

I burst out laughing for at least the fourth time in the short conversation we were having. My brother was many things, but humble was not one of them. The guy was a pussy magnet, and he knew it. We all had similar looks, but Law had charisma that was off the charts. Swagger would be more appropriate. He could talk to anyone, anywhere, about anything. He was more comfortable in his skin than anyone I'd ever met. The ladies loved his confidence and his genuine enjoyment of life.

"How do you know she's not after your trust fund? Or gaining new followers on her social media account by harvesting yours?" I introduced the ideas while traffic slowed to a maddening speed.

Shit . . . now I sounded like our father.

I was about three exits away from where I needed to get off the freeway, and if things slowed down more, I'd be late. This visit was already going to be miserable. I didn't need more stacked against me.

"I don't give a shit about any of that," Law said, shaking me from my worrying. "I just want to have a good time with the girl. If she thinks she's going to use me to land on the society page, she'll show her hand quick, and I'll cut bait."

"Have you asked her out?"

"Nope. We haven't spoken an actual word yet. Just been eye fucking across the gym all week." Then, in true Lawrence fashion, he switched topics midstride. "So why are you going to Mom and Dad's? Everything okay?"

It was a reasonable question for him to ask. Law knew I didn't hang out with our folks unless I had to.

Christ. How was I going to say this and not cause the guy to have a traffic accident?

"Listen. I need to tell you something, and it's pretty heavy," I warned. "I don't want you to flip your shit and run off the road."

"Oh boy, I can't wait to hear this," my brother said. "Lay it on me, man."

"I'm serious, Law. It's big." I paused for a second and quickly added, "I know your immature humor is dying to come out and play right now, but this is serious time."

"Oh my fucking God, Jacob. Just spit it out already and stop being so damn melodramatic."

"I have a child. A daughter."

There. How's that for dramatic, asshole?

"Come again?" was all he said in response after dead air hung between our two ends of the call for so long I thought I'd dropped him.

"Did you really not hear me, or can you not process what I told you?" I never knew with this guy. He had the attention span of a toddler. Especially if a woman walked by while he was having a conversation with someone.

"Don't fuck around like that, man. I thought you were

serious just then," he playfully threatened with a forced laugh. "Your voice was so solemn when you just said you have a fucking kid." Law rattled off the reply with all the glibness I expected he would.

"Because I'm not joking. Do you remember that woman I dated in school? Was head over heels for her?" I jogged his memory of my years in San Francisco.

"Yeah, then you went to Spain and she dumped your ass. Shit, I've never seen you so depressed in our whole lives like you were over that piece."

"Do not call the mother of my child a piece, Lawrence," I warned in my deepest, most solemn tone as I exited the freeway.

"Wait..." he said, and a moment went by. He must have been trying to work out the details but couldn't make sense of the situation with the few he had. "You better go back to the beginning and tell me the whole story. I thought you looked for that chick everywhere and never found her."

"I'm going to have to fill in the backstory later. I just got off the freeway, and I need to mentally psych myself up for what I'm about to do here."

"Dude, I don't envy you. The old man is going to blow a gasket."

As if I didn't already know.

Law whistled long and low on his end of the line. "Let's grab a beer when you get out of there. You can explain the whole shit show to me."

"Can't. I need to get back as soon as I can."

"Get back? What does that mean? Your baby mama already has you on a short leash? Shit, Jake, that didn't take long."

"There's more to the story, but I don't want to get into it before I pull up to the house. Seriously, though—" I began that final thought and then just stopped talking.

Now that I was on the old neighborhood streets, the memories from growing up in this area were fucking with my head. The same way they always did. For so many reasons, I wished my brother were sitting in my car with me, about to face our parents as a team. Like we did when we were mischievous boys finding trouble wherever we could. They always went easier on us when we got in trouble together.

"All right, where'd you just go, space cadet?" Law shook me from my anxious thoughts with his smart-ass remark.

But I'd spare him from the constant turmoil that swirled inside my head, so I skipped over the anxiety I always dealt with when I came back home and went straight for the bitterness. The two feelings were usually a package deal. Why would this visit be any different?

"Ahhh, you know, Law. Just stressing the fuck out. I'm so not in the mood for Dad's bullshit. You would think by this age, he'd respect me enough as a man to listen with an open mind and, God forbid, support me."

"You always were a dreamer, Jake," Law said, and even though the comment was snarky, I knew it was his way of letting me know he understood exactly what I was bitching about. "Call me when you can, brother."

"Thanks, Law. I will."

We hung up just as I pulled into the driveway of my family home. It was majestic and ostentatious at the same time. Huge because we needed the space, and grand because they could afford to have it that way. When I lived here, I rarely had friends over because I couldn't stand all the *ooohhs* and *aaahhs* and the twenty thousand questions that followed.

"What did you say your dad does for a living again?"

"How many cars are in your garage?"

"Do you know other famous people?"

And the crazy part about that was that these were equally wealthy kids from the same private school my siblings and I attended. Everyone in that academy had a pedigree of some type. Yet they still found my family interesting. Never could figure out why.

Granted, my mother was a stunning woman. She was a fashion model before my father started knocking her up over and over again. To this day, she had a killer figure and looked at least ten years younger than she was. She dressed in the latest styles, and designers loved when she wore their creations and was photographed. She was a society girl through and through but had the heart of a down-home girl. She and my father were always getting decked out and going to some charity ball or political fundraiser.

My father had always been a vain man. He kept in shape by drinking most of his meals instead of actually sitting down with the family for a shared supper. While he belonged to the local athletic club, it was more for show and status than physical fitness. The man did love the golf course, though, and actually had an enviable handicap.

Two of the three family greyhounds sprinted across the lawn to meet me on the driveway. The third, and oldest of the bunch, Callie, trotted along behind. Even now that she was getting up there in age, she did her best to keep up with her younger brothers, Milo and Morley.

Don't ask me—my youngest sister named them.

I squatted down to greet the animals, giving them all equal

time. Until, of course, I heard my mother's kind voice calling from the front walk.

"Jacob, is that you? I didn't see you pull up. But these darn dogs insisted on going out," she laughed as she came around the bend and into view.

"Hello, darling," she said with her arms open for an embrace.

I squeezed her gently and smiled. She'd always worn the same perfume—since I was a little boy—and it flooded my heart and mind with memories.

"Hi, Mom. Looking fabulous as always."

"Oh, *pffttt*," she said and swatted at my shoulder. But I knew she loved hearing it. "I'm so happy to see you. We've barely had any time since you moved back. Can we fix that?" she asked with a dramatic pout.

"I'm on a really big project at the moment. I barely have time for anything social," I explained. It wasn't a lie.

"Really? Already? Tell me all about it," my mom cooed as we strolled through the house to the formal living room. She had her arm hooked in mine and listened to me talk like I was truly interesting.

"Is Dad here? I really hoped to speak to both of you at the same time," I answered instead of more chit chat. I wanted to make this as quick as possible so I could get back to Calabasas.

"He was just finishing up with his weekly massage. I'm sure he'll be along any minute."

We sat down on the terribly uncomfortable furniture— she in her favorite chair and me on the long sofa. Oftentimes, she sat in this room and worked on her needlepoint because it had the best natural light. I looked around the space and really took in the decor. The contrast between the house I'd been staying at the past few days and this one was incredible.

Pia was a very wealthy woman. Even if she didn't benefit from being a major shareholder in her brother's company, she had a very successful career of her own. But her house felt like a home. The furniture sucked you in and wouldn't let go. The walls had the wear and tear of a child living within. This place looked like a damn museum.

Or maybe mausoleum.

My father's baritone voice snapped my attention back as he entered the room. "Jacob, son! To what do we owe the pleasure?"

"Hey, Dad." I quickly stood to greet him, and the man thrust his hand toward me. No hugs for this guy.

"Oh, Daniel, don't be like that," my mother chastised.

I hadn't missed his dig but chose to gloss over it instead. I wasn't here for a confrontation. Not today, at least.

"Can we sit down for a few minutes? I won't keep you long, but I have some exciting news to share, and I wanted you to hear it from me." I quickly took my place on the sofa and rubbed my sweaty palms on my thighs.

My parents took their his and hers wingbacks across from me. A giant silk flower centerpiece towered over the coffee table between us. I got lost for a few beats staring at the thing, wondering who the hell ever thought something like that looked better than a live, fresh bouquet.

"So, darling, what's this all about?" my mom asked before my father said something shitty.

"I'm not sure how to start this whole story, so I think just getting to the point will be the best approach. I can fill in the details after I rip the bandage off, so to speak."

"Well, get on with it, then," my father groused and shifted

his weight on the uncomfortable seat.

"Okay. Well..." I took a deep breath to steady my voice, not sure it helped at all.

My father's eyebrows hiked up a little higher as he was already losing patience.

"I've recently found out I have a child. A daughter. She's delightful and beautiful. Mom, you're going to just love her. She's nine. Well, almost nine."

"What the—" Dad grumbled.

"Oh, goodness." My mom clasped her hands in front of her chin. "A little girl. And she's Stella's age."

"She actually goes to school with Stella," I added. Seemed like a good point to make for some reason. I knew how much my folks cherished my niece, so connecting my daughter to her in any way could only help my cause.

"I'm not following," my father interrupted. "You said you just found this out? Where has the child been?"

"She lives here in Los Angeles. In Calabasas," I added and then rushed to say more. "Do you remember the girl I dated in school? You never met her, but I'm sure I talked about her all the time. We dated almost the entire four years we were there. But when I took the internship in Barcelona, she cut off all communication. Turns out, she did that because she was pregnant and didn't want to derail my career plans."

"Surely you've insisted on a DNA test," my father said.

"It's not necessary," I started to explain, but he scoffed like I was the village idiot.

"Of course it's necessary. Son, when you come from a prominent bloodline, people come out of the woodwork your entire life to suck you dry. Don't be a fool."

"She is the spitting image of me. It's uncanny, actually."

The grin spreading across my lips couldn't be held back.

"Still, darling, maybe it would be wise to know for sure. Sometimes young women see men in your position as an opportunity," my mom said in her gentle, birdsong tone, as if she were explaining the evil ways of the world to a naïve child.

Normally I found her voice to be comforting, but not then. I was a dead man if she took up sides with my father. My anxiety clicked up a notch right alongside my annoyance at being spoken to as though I was clueless.

"Who is the woman?" my dad barked while pulling out his phone.

"What are you doing?" I asked with a flick of my chin toward the device.

"I'm going to have my team investigate her. What do you think? If you're not going to protect your name and your assets, I'll have to do it for you."

The room felt like the furnace switched on until I rationalized it was my frustration raising my blood pressure and body temperature.

"I guarantee she is not after my money. She's a very wealthy, prominent woman herself. She doesn't need the Masterson name for that. In fact, she refuses to change her name or our daughter's when we marry."

"Oh?" From her pinched facial expression and that one word, I knew Mom didn't like that bit of news. The woman was all about tradition and family tree shit. "And you've already proposed? How long have you known about this?"

I knew this conversation would go south pretty fast, but this was quicker than even I expected. Maybe I should've brought Pia with me after all.

"You can't be serious, Jacob." My dad scowled. "Screw your damn head on, boy."

Thinking more details would help, I continued as if neither of them had spoken. "Her name is Cassiopeia Shark, and our daughter's name is Vela. She's eight, almost nine, and she's the most clever and intelligent child I've ever met. Pia has done a magnificent job raising her so far." Pride swelled from my heart and out through my words.

"Shark, you said?" He was connecting mental dots then, but I had no idea what he thought of Bas.

"Any relation to the freight mogul? The conceited ass building the skyscraper in the Financial District? Wait—that's the building you designed, isn't it?"

"Oh, dear, these are murky waters, aren't they?" my mom added.

I took a calming breath and tried to keep my head straight. When they fired question after question at me that way, I usually got overwhelmed and said something I shouldn't. But I didn't have anything to hide where my favorite girls were concerned, and I had to keep reminding myself of that. I wouldn't allow them to make me feel ashamed of what was going on in my life. These weren't even my decisions that landed me here in front of them.

"Yes, Sebastian Shark is her brother. Yes, I designed his building that is currently under construction. A project I'm very proud of, by the way, and there's already buzz about recognition from the AIA for my work." I spewed all of those facts out without taking a single breath. If I left a gap in the conversation, one of them would likely fire another question my way.

Of course, my mentioning the award buzz went in one ear and out the other. If that were one of my siblings, my mother would've already notified the entire bloodline in our family chat loop.

Being the black sheep really sucked sometimes. Just because I'd chosen a different career path outside the family business, my accomplishments had always been discredited. By this age, I was truly fed up with it. I hated the way they made me feel like I wasn't good enough. Never as good as Park or Cecile. Or any of the others. It was bullshit.

Now I pictured Pia standing up for me to my folks, had she come along. It would be great entertainment to witness my dad and her go toe to toe. Not that I would ever subject her to that. The man was just shy of a misogynist, and I would never allow him to disrespect my woman.

Silence blanketed the sitting room, and my mother fussed with the hem of her dress in discomfort. My dad had paced to the window and stared out to the front lawn for several minutes.

Finally, Mom asked, "Well, when can we meet them? Why didn't you bring them with you today? Seems like you're planning on becoming one big happy family."

"There's a lot going on right now." I tried to find the right way to explain the next part. "A lot of dangerous things."

"Dangerous?" they both repeated in chorus.

Now I was the one fascinated with my lap. How the hell did I explain the situation we were dealing with? The truth seemed to be the only choice, but when I went over the sparse details we had in my mind, the whole mess sounded like a movie trailer.

Without meeting either of their gazes, I said, "After school yesterday, an unauthorized stranger picked her up, and she's been missing since."

"Jacob! No! Have you called the police? Surely you've

called the police." My mother was up on her feet and pacing at once.

If there was one thing the woman excelled at, it was crisis management. I guessed after having ten kids, it became a way of life.

CHAPTER NINE

PIA

"Where's junior?" Elijah asked while setting up his laptop.

"Probably still in bed," Grant answered before I could.

"Stayed up past his bedtime last night," Bas grumbled as he walked back into the dining room from the kitchen. A steaming mug of coffee in each hand, he shoved one in my direction.

"You look like shit, Dub," he said with the offering.

I had a strong urge to dump the burning-hot brew down the front of his crisp dress shirt. I totally wasn't in the right frame of mind for their ribbing this morning.

"You know what? And this goes for the three of you," I said sternly while individually pointing from one to the other. "I'm not in the mood for your childish bullshit today. Neither of us slept well because our child is *missing*." The *ess* sound in the word came out on a bitter hiss. "Can you put yourself in my shoes for a minute and cut me some fucking slack?"

"Down girl," Bas said from over the rim of his mug.

Yeah, I really wanted to knock the thing right out of his hand.

"You know we're all doing the best we can to help," Elijah said.

"Sorry, Pia." Grant pulled me into his body for a sweet hug.

"No, I'm sorry." Rubbing my already tense forehead, I beseeched, "How am I going to survive if we don't get her back? She's my everything." Tears wet my cheeks the moment I allowed my anger to ebb. When I wasn't specifically feeling another emotion, my overwhelming despair took center stage.

"In all seriousness," Elijah said, "where is Jacob this morning?"

"He went to speak to his parents. Up until this morning, they still didn't know about Vela, or . . . well, me to any great extent."

I choked on the last couple of words but couldn't put my finger on why. It felt a lot like embarrassment, but that didn't make sense when I examined it. Probably the fact that we dated for years in college but I'd never even met the people. Because I certainly wasn't embarrassed to be with Jake. Not then and not now. He was textbook tall, dark, and handsome. More than that, actually. The man was smart, creative, kind, caring, and so much more. A smile took over my lips then, and I must have looked like I was losing it to the small audience staring at me. From tears to smitten in eight seconds flat.

"I wish you had talked to me before deciding to do that," my friend said. His icy green eyes were missing their usual brilliance.

I didn't realize we weren't the only two that had lost zee's last night.

"You guys have to stop this," I said with a heap of frustration. Before they could defend their meddling propensities, I went on. "Seriously! I know you all care for me like I am your flesh and blood, and I love you with all my heart for that and so many other reasons. But you have to stay in your own lane here. Let me make my own decisions—my own mistakes." With my hands propped on my hips, my defiant and defensive posture should have warned them to tread carefully.

Elijah widened his eyes and tipped his head toward his shoulder, and a chunk of sandy-colored hair fell in front of his eye. A practiced head toss cleared the strands from blocking his sight, and he took a deep breath.

"What I was going to say was, I wish you had talked to me first because I think it's imperative we continue to keep the authorities out of this. The moment these facts are repeated at a police station, over a scanner, or switchboard, all hell will break loose with the media."

"Jacob knows that—"

"But does he, Pia?" Sebastian interrupted. "I mean, *really*? How can you be sure he does?"

"Sebastian, excuse me. I was talking and you didn't let me finish." I narrowed my eyes his way. He could be so pushy and rude. "Christ. Now I don't even know what I was saying." I cradled my face in my palms and could feel the heat of my embarrassment and frustration. The two made a maddening cocktail.

Grant piped up. "You were explaining that Jake can handle his parents."

"Yes! Thank you. And that's actually a great way of saying it. Plus, you all know that family is no stranger to media scrutiny. I'm sure they understand how sensitive this is."

My brother groaned his disagreement. "I'm not worried about his family. I'm sure they have a team of PR people and lawyers that spoon feed them every sound bite we ever get from that camp."

My surly mood and nonexistent patience made my fuse very short this morning. "What's the actual problem here, brother? Just spit it out instead of condemning a man who doesn't deserve your negativity and lack of confidence." My voice's volume spiked with my anger.

"Hey, hey . . . " A new voice entered the conversation. "It's too early to be arguing already. Not to mention, acting like a bunch of eight-year-olds is the least productive way to bring the actual eight-year-old back home," Wren reminded us in lieu of a normal morning greeting. My assistant gave me a long hug and, when we parted, asked, "Did you sleep? A little at least?"

"Off and on," I replied. "What about you? How are you feeling this morning? Are you having pain?"

Every time I was reminded the woman had been in a car accident the day before, I was flooded with guilt. It was unfair that the seriousness of her experience was being overshadowed by Vela's abduction.

Abduction. That word snaked through my mind and, like a constrictor, pressed on my airway until I was close to panicking. Wren scrutinized my physical state and muttered quietly so the boys didn't hear, "Hey are you okay? All of a sudden, you're white as a sheet."

I gave her a quick shake of my head, hoping she understood to drop it. While I appreciated her concern, I knew I could not tolerate my brother's bull-in-a-china-shop version of the same thing. If he clued into me not being the picture of perfect health, he'd have me lying on the sofa and sidelined from today's search plans.

"Excuse me for a minute," I said in the strongest voice I could gather. When the men stopped talking and looked my way, I said, "I need to call Jake. I'm going to do that from my bedroom." Then I dashed off before any of them felt like they needed to offer an opinion about my actions. Was there such a thing as *too close* to the ones you loved? Without a doubt, *too comfortable* was very real and present.

In my room, I leaned my back against the closed door and slid down until my butt hit the floor. My legs were shaky, and stars danced in front of my eyes. I needed to test my blood sugar and probably get more in my stomach than a cup of coffee. Or three.

I dialed Jake's number with a trembling hand and listened to the call ring out. His deep, serious, businessman voice filled my ears and flowed through my whole body like melted chocolate. With closed eyes, I listened to his voicemail greeting and let his comforting tone soothe me. If I couldn't speak to him directly, I'd settle for this instead.

"Hey, it's me. I was just checking to see how it went with your parents and—and—well, I just really wanted to hear your voice." I paused for a long moment and finished by saying, "Well, anyway, call me when you can. Bye."

Ending the call, I locked the screen on my device and froze. Vela's innocent face stared up at me from the background wallpaper and through my apps. It was a picture I'd snapped of her over the summer while swimming at Sebastian's house. She wore a huge smile, and the splash of freckles that came out in the sunshine were on full display. I could remember that day as though it was yesterday.

Christ, how I wished it was. If we could've gone back in time, just to the hour before this nightmare began, I'd pick her up at school and listen to her prattle on about whatever she'd been into that day.

The pain in my chest became unbearable as I sat there. I had to find her, had to bring her home. But in that moment, I couldn't do anything but sob. I wilted to the floor completely, lay on my side, drew my knees up to my chest, and cried. Image after image of her with those bright blue eyes assaulted my mind. The child was always so full of wonder and ready to pepper anyone within earshot with twenty-six questions about as many random topics.

Not sure how long I curled up there, but a sizable wet spot formed on the carpet from the tears that rolled down my face and plopped to the floor.

The soft knock startled me at first, and I quickly sat up and dashed the tears from my face. The knock came again, this time a bit louder, and Wren added, "Pia? You okay in there?"

My voice was thick and husky with emotion when I tried to answer. "Yeah." I cleared my throat with a muffled cough and tried again. "Yeah, I'm good."

Without invitation, she turned the handle and pushed the door until it knocked into me.

"Oh, shit. I'm sorry," she stammered. "I didn't realize you were right there."

"Don't worry about it. It just bumped me. All good," I said with a fake, brittle smile.

"You're the worst liar. You know that, right?" she asked with a grin as genuine as mine was manufactured.

"I feel like I'm dying inside, Wren. I won't survive this if we don't find her."

"We're going to find her. From what I can pick up from the conversation out there"—she gestured toward the dining room where the men were gathered—"this has nothing to do with her and everything to do with your brother."

"Is there new information? What's making them say that?" I rushed toward her, and she looked alarmed by my sudden movement. "Sorry. Sorry. I didn't mean to freak you out," I quickly apologized, again feeling like a total shit.

In the middle of the drama swamp of my own existence, I completely forgot about the psychological scars my dear friend wore inside her heart and mind. On a normal day—*Ha! What the hell did normal look like anymore?*—I was typically very cognizant of Wren's triggers.

I couldn't stop myself from apologizing a second time. "I'm truly sorry, Wren. You know my mind isn't in the best shape at the moment."

Wren frowned. "Give yourself the same grace you extend to others, please. Isn't that what you always preach to me?" She raised a brow and stared, knowing damn well she'd gotten me good with that singular point.

"Yes. Yes, I tell you that all the time. Good to know someone pays attention when I speak."

She gave me a quick wink and said, "Not always, though. So don't get your hopes up too high."

Now I playfully shoved her toward the door. "Let's go see what the guys have in the way of a plan. I can't sit here all day and wait for that nutjob to call again. I'll be just as nutty by sunset if that's what they propose."

"Well, based on the amount of testosterone wafting out from that room, there's no way a plan they come up with is going to involve you."

"We'll see about that," I warned as we went down the hall arm in arm.

★ ★ ★

"Absolutely not," my bully brother said. The man's thickly

muscled arms were crossed over his broad chest while his blue eyes became narrow slits.

"Bas, you're not being reasonable," I said in a calm tone. *I would be nominated for some sort of sainthood if I didn't smack him soon.* "And here's another fact that seems to have been lost in that control-freak mind of yours. I do not require your approval of anything I do. Those days are long gone, and if I want to go outside of this house to search for my missing child, that's exactly what I'll do." I leaned one hip against the dining room table and mirrored his stubborn stare.

"Cassiope—" he started, but I held up my hand to stop him.

"Oh, no you don't. Not the full-name bullshit right now, Bas."

"I don't know how else to make sure you're listening to me!" my sibling bellowed. "We don't need to worry about another abduction right now!" His voice thundered louder with each point he insisted on making. "We need to be concentrating all our efforts on finding Vela! If you go out there . . . "

In my peripheral vision, I saw Wren shrinking back into the corner. My dumbass brother was checking off every box on her trigger list with his tyrannical behavior. Luckily, Grant noticed what was happening and stepped in.

"Okay, let's calm down. The yelling isn't necessary . . . " the tall guy said while holding his arms out like a priest blessing his parish.

I maintained the stare-down with my brother while his best friend played peacemaker. I knew we needed to modulate our voices, but I would not be silenced completely.

"Do you hear yourself? If I go out there? Sebastian, this is Calabasas, not the frontline of a Baghdad skirmish." Through flared nostrils, I sucked in a lungful of air to try and calm down. Damn it, where was Jake? He'd be on my side in this stupid argument.

After glancing at my assistant again and taking stock of her physical state, I silently vowed to dial down my aggravation. It wasn't fair to any of the other people in the room to have to witness a sibling squabble on top of everything else they were already giving up for us. I went to where she was subtly trembling in the corner of the dining room and took her in my arms.

Very quietly, I said, "I'm sorry. No more yelling, I promise. I'm being a shit friend right now and very selfish. Please forgive me for being so self-centered."

She pulled back from my embrace just a bit and replied. "You are none of those things. Stop it. My issues are my issues. I understand that. I'm working very hard to get on top of the bullshit I was handed, you know?"

"I know you are, and I'm so proud of you," I praised, but she cut me off there.

"But this isn't about me right now, so please...focus on bringing our girl home." She darted her eyes toward my brother across the room and then back to me. For my ears only, she muttered, "He's being a controlling ass right now. He won't even let you explain what you had in mind while out in the neighborhood."

"I know, and he's driving me crazy," I said just as quietly. "But I also know it's out of love and loyalty. Habits as old as his regarding caring for me are hard to just turn off."

"And you are silly enough to call yourself self-centered." The young woman shook her head with a heavy dose of bewilderment. "You are understanding and empathetic even when everyone else should be handling you with kid gloves."

"Oh, yes, and I'd respond well to that, too," I said, and we both laughed then, knowing the level of sarcasm involved in that one little comment.

Precisely then, my front door swung open, and my gorgeous man strode in. I pretended not to hear the grumblings from the other men about knocking or something about having a key. Instead, I hurried to the foyer to greet him.

His arms were the only place I wanted to be. Right then and possibly forever. I knew my heart and soul were in a very vulnerable place at the moment, so I had to be careful not to say anything or commit to anything permanent until we had this situation under control.

I was just too raw and too ready for a giant dose of TLC. If I thought Jacob was the kind of man who would take advantage of a woman in a compromised state, I would never have been with him in the first place.

So far, he'd been nothing but supportive and loving. He had given me the space to cry and exhaust my fears, and I needed to remind myself he may be needing those same things. Again, I considered how selfish I'd been behaving.

True, the man hadn't had much time to spend with our daughter, but astonishingly, they had already formed a lovely bond. I was excited when I allowed myself to daydream about the future, to imagine what our family might be like. When this dust settled, we'd have to be extra patient with each other, and with Vela, because there was no way to predict what her residual scars would look like. I couldn't be happier that those were waters I wouldn't have to navigate alone.

"How did it go?" I rushed out the question while still in his embrace.

"Pretty much as expected."

"Explain," I urged then winced. My brother's catchphrase flowed from my mouth as though it were my own.

Jacob just raised a single brow while staring down at me. "Well, as you can imagine, they weren't happy that I'd kept this from them," he answered with a frown. "And I tried to explain as concisely as possible while still preserving your honor. I just don't think they are very forgiving people. They never really have been."

"My honor?" I pushed from his embrace and instantly went into a defensive stance. "What is that supposed to mean?"

But it took a lot to rattle this man. My pissy attitude didn't touch his resolve. Or his patience, which I probably didn't deserve at that point.

He calmly inhaled deeply. "Think about it, Star. How would you explain the situation without making you sound like the bad guy here? But I think I handled it pretty well." He seemed pleased with himself, and I could feel my ire sparking up again.

And if I really took a moment to examine my feelings about what he said, I would recognize the guilt for what it was. Instead, I shifted into combat mode and tried to think of any verbal ammunition I had in my arsenal.

But nope, my bunker was empty. He was right—the only reason he missed almost nine years of his daughter's childhood was because I made choices for him that I had no right to make.

"I'm so sorry," I said and hung my head in shame.

Jacob lifted my gaze back to his with one steady finger beneath my chin. "Why are you apologizing?" His kind eyes searched my face for any hint of what I was thinking.

"Because I know I'm the one who created this situation

for you. I'm sorry if it made more trouble between you and your parents. I hope you realize, at the very least, when I chose to not tell you about the pregnancy all those years ago, I never once considered how many people would be robbed of time with her." I dropped my eyes as he still held my face. "I can't apologize enough."

"Sit with me a moment," he said and tugged us to the formal sitting area I had just inside the front door. No one ever came into this room unless I was hosting a party or gathering that extended past my family. The furniture was uncomfortable and the decor stuffy, and the more I looked around the room, the more I wondered what the hell I was thinking when I designed it. Maybe I'd tackle a redo for something fun to focus on.

Of course, after we got our daughter back. Because outside of that one objective, it was difficult to concentrate on anything else. And if I did have a moment of freedom from the nonstop panic about her safety and general well-being, I immediately felt guilty for thinking about something else.

Jacob angled his body toward mine and offered his open hands to me. Not sure what was happening, I just stared at them for a few seconds. Maybe he was going to tell me he changed his mind and wanted to take her from me. Maybe after talking to his parents, he decided he didn't want to try to be a family, or maybe they insisted he not stay with us.

"Cass." His deep, dominant voice jolted me out of the freak-out I was spinning up.

I met his stare and couldn't read his expression.

"Please let me hold your hands. I missed you while I was apart from you. Even for that short time." He smiled and gave his head a slight shake. "Do I sound pathetic or what?"

I placed my hands in his, feeling like ten times the jerk

for letting my mind sabotage me the way it had. Normally, I was so much better at shutting down the negative self-talk. To say I wasn't operating at prime, though, would be an epic understatement.

"That's not pathetic. It's sweet. Thank you for telling me that. I was getting myself all worked up in my mind that you pulled me in here to dump me or something," I admitted while staring at our entwined hands. I couldn't look him in the eye just yet. My heart was still trying to catch up with my head.

"No, darling. You ladies are stuck with me now." His warm smile melted my heart. "I wanted to put an end to your apologizing. When I decided to put all my chips in the kitty, so to speak, it was in part by promising myself to leave the past in the past. I vow to you, I won't bring that shit up, throw it in your face, guilt you about it—anything. What's done is done."

"Jake—"

"No, let me finish. I want to be sure to get all this out. I've been thinking about it a lot. You. Me. Our daughter. Our future. You and I have years of amazing memories that I don't want to lose or disrespect by focusing on the negative. Life is too precious, too abundant, to obsess over the bad shit. You know?"

Again, unwelcomed tears streaked down my cheeks and around my jaw. How were there any left at this point? Jacob released my hands to tenderly swipe my cheeks with his thumbs. While cradling my face, he leaned in for a soft kiss.

"Just a little salty today," he said with a twinkle in his eyes.

"Do you know how much I love you?" I croaked. Was it too soon to fall back into admitting these heavy feelings with a man I hadn't seen for the better part of a decade? My heart and soul didn't think so. Because I'd never stopped loving him in the first place.

His expression dropped at once, and I panicked that I'd jumped the gun. Maybe he wasn't feeling the same way. It was too late to recall the sentiment, though. There wasn't an option to say I was just joking. Not that I'd ever been the type of person to joke about emotions. I barely acknowledged the things that affected me or those around me.

After countless hours with my therapist, I knew why that twisted mindset existed. I knew that I was always in various stages of emotional unavailability. I had my mind—and my heart—trained to believe the only thing that came from being emotionally vulnerable around someone else was pain.

Not necessarily the physical kind, but the psychological kind, which, in my opinion, hurt way worse than visible cuts and bruises. Those would heal. Emotional pain wasn't curable. The best you could hope for was that it would fade with time.

Thankfully, my handsome man didn't make me swim in my pool of fear for long. He saw the panic setting in and quickly squashed my worry.

"I've been tripping over those same words for a few days. Hell, since the moment I first saw you again in your brother's office. Thank you for being brave enough to say them out loud. I love you too. I love everything about you. All the things I know and all the things I'm still to discover. I love our past, and our future, and I'm so ready to put this shitty drama behind us and finally have the happiness we deserve." He ended that declaration with a deep, passionate kiss that left me breathless.

"I've been waiting for you for so long," I whispered and held his palms to my cheeks.

"And I'm so honored by your devotion, Star. Beyond what words can describe. Now, let's bring our girl home."

CHAPTER TEN

JACOB

The call we'd been waiting for finally came. This time, Sebastian's phone rang, and the whole room fell silent.

Several conversations had been swarming around the space until that paralyzing ring came from his cell phone. He waited for a nod from Elijah, who immediately dashed to his open laptop. Apparently he possessed some sort of call-tracking software that he and his team used routinely and had droned on for long moments about its sophistication and accuracy.

None of that mattered to me or my daughter's mother— we just wanted Vela returned safely. However it happened, that was our sole focus.

"Shark," Sebastian barked toward his phone. He set the device on the dining room table, and we all stared at it like the thing was a live grenade.

"Hello, brother," a creepy voice hissed through the speaker. A shiver racked my entire body just thinking this son of a bitch had my child.

"Listen, fucker, I don't have a brother, so stop fucking around and tell us what you want."

Elijah and Grant both shot Bas censuring glares, but the man's eyes were narrow slits focused directly on his mobile.

"Oh, careful now, dear brother," the bastard said in an irritating sing-song voice. "That temper of yours is going to just make things harder for our niece."

"Let me speak to my daughter. Right now!" Pia shouted at the phone as if it were the culprit himself.

"Hello, sister of mine. It would appear a short fuse is in our genetic makeup." The creep followed that statement with a sickening laugh. If Sebastian didn't tear this asshole apart, Pia surely would.

"Cut the bullshit, man. Tell us what you want in exchange for the child. Actually, you're going to have to first prove she's there and well, or there will be no deal at all," Shark threatened.

"Now there you go again, thinking you have the upper hand. I know you're used to that, brother, but this time you'll have to get used to taking the orders."

We all just stared at the phone, waiting for this guy to get to the point.

Sebastian was as angry as Pia was worried. The man stood with his thick arms crossed defiantly over his chest while my beautiful star paced back and forth along the dining room table. Her agitation was ramping up my own, so when she passed by me for the third time, I snaked my arm around her waist and pulled her into my body. She was trembling so hard, her vibrations traveled through my body too.

Very quietly, I whispered, "Calm down, darling. I'm sure she's fine. This guy can't be that stupid. Ask him where he wants to meet. I don't think your brother can think straight right now."

She gave a quick nod and pulled from my embrace. "Tell us where you want to meet. We'll give you whatever you want in exchange for her safe return." My woman looked to me after issuing the demand, and I nodded in approval. Even though the situation was complete shit, my heart swelled because she sought me out in the room filled with so many close loved ones.

"I assume you're familiar with the Port of Long Beach?" the man asked.

"Of course I am," Bas scoffed. "Have you really not done your homework? Do you know who I am?" Bas bit his reply as Elijah mimed a slice across his own throat. I could only assume he was telling him to temper his attitude with that gesture, and I wanted to hug him for interjecting. There was no place for the man's gigantic ego in this conversation.

"Oh, I know all there is to know about you, Sebastian Albert Shark. I've been planning for the day we finally came face to face for decades."

"Christ, get a life, man," Grant muttered under his breath, and Pia shot him a look while shaking her head.

I doubt the dude even heard what Twombley said, but she was right. We didn't need to piss him off unnecessarily.

Bas spoke in the direction of the phone again. "The port is massive. Exactly where on the property do you want to meet?"

"Follow the bike path on Pier J to the very end. I'll be waiting for you there. Arrive at exactly eight thirty-two tonight. If you know why that time is of such significance, I'll send you a picture of the girl. You have two minutes to come up with the reason."

Pia and Sebastian looked at each other, and both threw their hands up. Okay, clearly they didn't know what this lunatic was talking about, but we needed to figure it out so we could see proof our daughter was in good shape. I quickly dashed over to an open laptop on the dining room table and did an internet search for the date and time stamp.

Pia crowded in behind me to see what my search netted. "Does any of this look relevant?" I asked her over my shoulder. When she didn't answer, I turned more in my chair to watch her eyes scan back and forth over the entries.

And then she jolted upright and snapped her face toward her brother. She mouthed, *Is this his birthday? Caleb's, I mean.*

"I don't fucking know," he growled under his breath.

"Tick tock, siblings!" the asshole crooned over the line. "One minute remaining."

Across the table from where I sat, Elijah was feverishly typing. "I got it here," he said without bothering to lower his volume. He met Sebastian's stare directly, and the two were motionless. Speechless, too.

I couldn't tell if I was creeped out or in awe of the level of friendship these people had. Watching a near telepathic conversation between the two men was odd and incredible at the same time.

When I looked to see Pia's reaction, she was locked in the same tractor beam her brother was. Well, shit. Looks like my woman spoke their secret language too. I'd definitely be getting the translation when we ended the phone call.

But I didn't have to wait that long. Sebastian stepped closer to the phone and said, "It's Caleb's birthdate and time. But anyone can look up public records, so don't think by having that bit of information we're convinced you are who you say you are."

"Now send the picture. If you are a Shark," Pia said while rolling her eyes, "you're a man of your word."

"Don't get high and mighty with me. Claiming the family name is the last thing on my mind," the man replied. "Be at Pier J as planned." And then we heard the telltale *beep beep*

beep that signaled the connection was cut.

"No!" Pia shouted and buried her face in her hands.

In a flash, I was on my feet and cradling her in my arms while she sobbed.

"Baby, sssshhhh. All right. All right." I hushed into her hair, keeping my lips against her overheated skin.

Just then, her phone signaled an incoming message, and everyone stilled at once. Pia pulled back from the comfort of my arms and unlocked her phone.

"Oh my God! Oh my God!" she said while her hand violently shook.

I crowded into her personal space and saw what she was freaking out about.

It was her. A picture of our daughter. Disheveled, dirty, and tear streaked, but she was okay. She didn't have visible bruises, and her eyes looked clear and focused. I held on to hope they hadn't drugged her.

"Thank God," I murmured and crushed Pia into my body. Her phone was pressed between our hearts while I held on to her shaking frame as much for my own comfort as to provide it in return.

"Look, she's okay. We'll get her back, Cass. It's going to be okay." I mumbled the same few things over and over and could recognize it was in part for my own convincing.

Pia fell into my chest again after one of the guys took the phone to see the photo. A conversation immediately erupted between the three best friends while Pia and I held on to each other in the corner. Her tears made a sizable wet patch on the front of my shirt. I reached in my back pocket for a handkerchief and handed it over.

When she finally calmed down, she asked, "Where is my phone? I want to look at that picture again."

"Dub, I need to try to trace this if that's okay?" Elijah held up the device while talking. "Why don't I forward the file to Cole's phone, and you can look at it there?"

Pia nodded quickly and then dabbed at her nose with my handkerchief. My phone dinged in my pocket.

"That was me," Elijah said. "Check to be sure it wasn't encrypted."

I stared at the screen for a long moment, happier than I could express that she was holding up. I was ashamed I didn't know my own child well enough to predict how she would handle a situation like the one she was in, so my relief was likely double everyone else's.

"What time is it?" Pia asked the entire group. "Should we go there now?"

Her brother was the one to speak up. "You're not going. None of you are. I'll go. And I'll bring our girl home."

"The hell I'm not!" Pia's voice rose at least one octave from panic. "Sebastian, I'm going," she repeated when he just stared at her.

"Jake, talk some sense into her. I need to call Abbigail and check on my family." And with that, the bossy man strode from the room. In a few moments, we heard the front door close behind him.

Pivoting toward Pia, I was met with a very defiant stare. She propped her hands on her hips in challenge as she geared up to mount her case. I inwardly cursed the motherfucker for starting this debate and then skating out of the room. Damn coward. He knew how feisty his sister was. And headstrong? Ha! That didn't even come close to being a strong enough descriptor for the woman.

"I'm going."

"Star, maybe he has a point," I began, but she widened her eyes with what I could only interpret as fury.

"I said, I'm going."

After a fortifying inhale, I said, "Yes, I heard what you said, but I think you should listen—"

She cut me off before I could finish my reasoning.

"I'm. Going," Pia repeated, and this time vocally stomped on each word.

Grant rounded the table to get in on the battle. "Pia, listen for a minute. Please."

"Don't you start too." She glared at the tall man.

"While that it is an impressive glare, darling, you're forgetting who my wife is," he said with a casual grin after mentioning Rio. "I'm just going to say it. What good will it do Vela if something happens to you?" he asked calmly. "Do you really want her to witness you getting injured?"

"Or worse," I added.

"How can I possibly sit here and wait while Sebastian handles this?" she whimpered.

"He *should* handle it!" I slammed my fist to the table, and all the items nearby hopped from the impact. My outburst resulted in all eyes turned my way. So I forged ahead. "Everything that has happened recently has been because of him. It's about time he cleans up his own mess." I couldn't hold back my anger now if I tried. I'd been diplomatic. I'd been patient. But now I was pissed, and I would not sit by and watch my love put herself in crosshairs meant for her brother.

Three people were already dead because of their association with the man. When would it be enough?

Instead of matching her tone and volume to my outburst, Pia calmly reasoned, "If by some strange course of events, this guy is really who he says he is—our brother, Caleb—it's as much my responsibility to clean up the mess, as you called it, as it is Sebastian's."

Grant shook his head in disbelief. "There's no way the guy is your dead brother. Do you have the infant's death certificate?"

My woman teared up again before admitting, "No. Of course we don't. Well, I don't at least. We were small children when he was born. We'll have to ask Bas when he comes back if he ever came across that when we lived in that crappy rental on the East Side."

"Elijah," I called because he was so engrossed in the work he was doing on his laptop. He hadn't stopped typing since he searched for Caleb's birth records.

"Can you find a death certificate for Caleb Shark?" I asked. "Should be public record, right?"

He finally lifted his brilliant stare to the room. He had been so focused on his work, he almost looked dazed when he realized he was in a room with other people.

"That's what I've been digging for since I found his birth certificate. I think you and Bas have said he died within hours of his birth. Is that right?"

"Well, as far as I know. Again, keep in mind I was three years old at the time. I don't remember the specifics of the event but heard the story recounted so many times since then, I believe those are the facts."

Grant went to lean over Elijah and look at his monitor. "What have you found, bro?"

Elijah leaned back in his chair and exhaled heavily. "That's just the problem. Nothing. I've found absolutely nothing regarding an infant dying that day. I've been looking at internal records from the three closest hospitals to that old house. The only infant death that day was a baby girl."

Then I asked, "How many hospitals are there in LA, though? I suppose it's possible they traveled to a different hospital."

"Right, so I'm expanding my search, hospital by hospital, outward from where that old dump was located," Banks explained and stretched his neck from one side to the other. "There's just a lot of data to review."

"How can we help?" the tall man offered as he sat beside his buddy at the table.

"Well, first I have to get into each hospital's server. Once I do that, we can swap places and you can scan the data for what we're looking for. Thanks for offering, man."

The good-natured guy wore his typical ear-to-ear grin. "Yeah, no worries. I've already been through the security footage from overnight, so I was ready for a new job."

For Cassiopeia's ears only, I asked, "Hey, where is your assistant? Maybe you should go check on her." While I understood that Pia knew the woman better than anyone in the house at the moment, it seemed a little unusual that the young woman chose that time to hide out in her room. Either that, or I was getting completely paranoid and thought everyone's actions seemed suspicious.

My girlfriend jolted from my embrace. Instantly, I felt like shit for worrying her. "See?" she asked by way of proving a point, it seemed. I just couldn't figure out what was meant by that one word. So she pressed on with an explanation. "This is another example of what I was talking about before. I am so selfish. I didn't even notice she'd been missing from the room all this time. What does that say about me?"

I took both her hands in mine and responded. "It says that you have a lot going on in your own life. Our daughter is missing. We're trying to work out a plan to get her back. None of those things make you selfish." With each comment, I crowded closer into her personal space. In a deep, dark tone, I said beside her ear, "I will stripe your ass if I hear you say that again."

Through narrowed eyes, I watched my words flow over her and cause several changes in her appearance. The look she gave me was a mixture of lust, need, and frustration. None of the other people in this room knew about her preferences—or at least I didn't think they did. Watching her try to school her reaction fortified my theory. I couldn't help but chuckle as she struggled to settle down. Though I would much rather observe her in this state than a few of the others I'd seen already today. Angry, sad, scared, and defiant could gladly be traded for her current, cock-swelling heated look.

I mouthed the words *pain slut* to her and grinned even wider as my words registered with her and she popped her eyes cartoonishly wide.

Pia gave a quick shrug to completely own the label.

My God, I loved this woman. I never stopped loving her while we were separated, either. We just needed the damn universe to cut us a break now and allow us to get our beautiful little girl back so we could start our happily ever after. Based on the warm emotion coursing through my body in that moment, I knew that was exactly what we'd have.

Especially since neither of us would settle for less.

Elijah spoke up again and snapped Pia and me out of our private moment. She excused herself to go speak with Wren, and I gave Banks my full attention. Now that she'd left the room, I needed a task to do too.

"I need to check in with my security team and bring the lead up to speed with tonight's plan. We're definitely going to need some backup." He paused and thought a moment.

"Good idea," I commented. "You know my family has an entire security staff as well. Do you feel like you have enough men? I'm sure I could round up at least another five or so who aren't on duty at the moment." I had to do something constructive, or I'd crawl out of my skin.

"You know what, Cole? Or Masterson... whatever. That's a good idea," he said while nodding. "See how many guys you can muster here in the next thirty minutes. That way we can all debrief and have a solid strategy going in. I'm going to make this call and then start scoping out the meeting spot via satellite so we can identify any potential problems."

"You got it," I said enthusiastically and already had my phone in my hand to call my father's guards. By the end of the phone conversation, I had the commitment of four extra men to help wherever we needed them. For now, I told the volunteers to come to Pia's address, and Elijah could dispatch them wherever he saw fit.

When Pia came out of Wren's room, she turned and very carefully closed the door. Her assistant didn't emerge with her, though, so I gestured a *what's up?* sort of motion.

"She's exhausted. I think we all keep forgetting she was in a car accident just two—or was it three days ago?" She looked to me for the answer, but at the moment, I had no better concept of time than anyone else in the room. It felt like I was living through the longest one day of my life.

Sebastian charged back into the room. I was convinced the man didn't have a casual bone in his body. He was like a furious storm with everything he did. Dude would have a heart attack by forty if he didn't find a way to relax a bit.

I totally understood the situation we were facing was tense and frightening—not that he'd ever admit to the latter—but the rest of us were in casual clothes, and he still wore slacks and a button down. Everyone else in the group had taken a turn on the sofa in the other room for a quick recharge, but not Shark. He sat with a ramrod spine and angrily tapped away on his laptop. Honestly, he reminded me a lot of my father. While their work ethic was completely admirable, that kind of intensity was difficult for others to be around for extended periods of time.

Well, it was for me, at least.

"How's Abbi doing?" Pia inquired.

"She says she's all right, but I don't think she's being honest with me. I think she's been having morning sickness and doesn't want to alarm me. But I've set up my home security system to ping me every time a bathroom door is engaged, and it's definitely increasing."

"Sebastian Albert!" Pia chided.

"What?"

She scowled while continuing to chastise her brother. "Have you stopped to think maybe that's why she hides stuff from you? You're a bit overbearing, don't you think?"

Only his sibling could get away with speaking to him that way. The rest of the witnesses in the room knew it too, based on the disbelieving way they all stared at the pair. Maybe waiting for him to blow up at her like he did everyone else who dared to challenge him?

But the man grinned instead and gave a quick nod. "Yeah, maybe you're right, Dub."

She went and gave him a quick squeeze from the side and matched her smile to his. "I know that kills you every time you have to admit it. Don't think your pain is lost on me, brother."

"Will you ever not be an annoying little sister?" Bas asked while looking down at his much smaller sibling.

"It's not looking like it, is it?"

"No. No it's not." Then he soundly clapped his hands together and addressed the room. "Where are we at? Is there a plan in place? Just tell me where you want me, Banks."

"I'll know that in a few minutes," Elijah answered without looking up.

I took the opportunity to explain what Sebastian missed while outside on the phone.

Wrapping up everything we knew so far, I said, "So he's looking at the area surrounding Pier J via satellite so we can strategically place the team."

"What team? I said I'm going in alone," Bas answered quickly and resolutely.

"We have Elijah's team plus a few on loan from Cole's family. Professionals," Grant explained. "There's no way any of us would stand by and be okay with you storming into that place without some sort of backup."

I couldn't help but notice how quiet Pia had become on the topic. She was definitely cooking something up in her mind, though. I could tell by the way she was miles away with her attention.

Quietly, I said, "Star?" And when she didn't so much as blink, I put my hand on her arm, causing her to startle. "Shit, girl. Where were you just then?"

"Sorry. I was . . . " But then she shook her head slightly and didn't finish her thought.

I stood in front of her, effectively blocking us from the rest of the room with my larger frame. I leaned in and kissed her temple and stayed that close to her when I asked, "What are you planning in that clever mind, darling?"

She tried incredulity first, and I narrowed my eyes at her acting. "Baby, I know you too well to bullshit. You should know that by now. Plus, I won't allow you to put yourself in harm's way. We need to trust the security team and believe they will bring our girl home to us."

Before speaking, she sucked in a big breath through her nose, so I quickly covered her mouth with mine. The whimper she released into my kiss shot straight to my dick, and the damn thing perked up instantly. After all these years, my body was so wired to her pain. Even that little sound of impending distress ramped me up.

Groaning in response, I really poured my soul into the kiss. I swept in deep with my tongue, and she sagged against me. In my mind, we had completely transported from that dining room with the small audience, and instead, I had this woman strung up on something—didn't matter what—and was preparing to give her what she needed. By my side, I clenched and released my fist, feeling the weight of her favorite belt in my hand.

My teeth found the cushion of her bottom lip and sank in until she moaned in surrender. I did my best to swallow her cry, but someone cleared his throat behind us, and I pulled back.

Pia took a few seconds to open her eyes, and they were my favorite, hooded and glassy.

"Tonight, Star, it is so on. You'll think of me every time you sit down tomorrow. Hell, every time you simply move."

"Mmmm, promise?"

With a slow grin, I shook my head. "So sassy these days, girl."

Pia jolted out of my arms, and I cautiously and curiously waited to hear what was on her mind.

"First, we get our child back. I shouldn't be thinking of anything but that right now." She shook her head and frowned, and I immediately pulled her back into my arms.

Into the silky waves of her hair, I said, "Give yourself some grace, please. We're going to get her back in just a few hours. I don't want to ever see you beating yourself up for expressing your own needs and desires. It's not wrong or bad to do that. To care for yourself too." I could feel her nodding in agreement before I pulled back to look into her beautiful face. "Now let's find out where we can help."

CHAPTER ELEVEN

PIA

Jacob was right. I knew he was, and I knew I was being ridiculous with my internal criticism, but some habits were harder to break than others. This one was a real doozy, but with this incredible, kind, compassionate, and giving man by my side, I felt like anything was possible.

This old habit was negative residue from having to go it alone for so long. I had to remind myself over and over that it wasn't the case now. I had a partner who wanted to share my life with me. Carry the burdens together and celebrate the milestones too. These were all the things my dreams were made of for the past nine years. Maybe pinching myself every now and then would ensure I was wide awake.

When we rejoined the conversation, I had trouble understanding what the guys were talking about.

"I don't know," Grant said. "The two don't seem to go together. At least for me they don't. You know? I can't draw a line connecting those two dots."

Elijah was busy swapping parts between two cell phones but added, "I don't think we should discount any possibility."

"What are you guys talking about?" I finally asked.

They all looked at Jacob, then me, then each other.

Well . . . hell. What was that all about?

Of course, Jacob noticed their behavior too. Seeming annoyed, he asked, "Do you need me to leave the room? Clearly whatever you're talking about doesn't involve me."

"Don't be ridiculous," I interrupted. "You're as much a part of this as I am. Vela is our child. That alone makes you family. And . . . " I took a steadying breath because I couldn't predict how all these protective men would react to what I was about to say.

"And what?" my brother barked.

I narrowed my eyes in his direction. His bossy crap was getting under my skin worse than normal.

"And I love Jacob. You all know that. You've known that for years. You just didn't know who he was. But if you all love Vela and me and care about us the way I think you do, you're going to have to accept that Jacob is part of our lives now. And forever will be."

My man stepped in behind me and put a possessive hand on my lower back. Just feeling his physical nearness gave me the fortitude to hold each one of their stares and prepare for their reactions.

Shockingly, there were no outbursts. No lists of reasons I was being foolish. Instead, Grant was the first to move. He stepped right into my personal space and wrapped me in a supportive, brotherly hug.

In my ear he said, "I'm happy for you, Pia. I want all the best for you and that little girl. If this is the guy to give you that, you have my full support."

Tears filled my eyes, and when I pulled back, I saw he was choked up too. That made me lose it completely. Why did seeing strong, dominant men show emotion strike me square in the heart? Every single time.

"Thank you," I croaked and watched him offer a hand to Jacob next.

"You take care of this one right here," he said while they shook. "Or you'll have to answer to all three of us." He finished with his trademark lazy grin, and it felt like another piece of my life's puzzle snapped into place.

Of course, Bas had to end the emotional moment. "All right, if we're done with the Kumbaya shit, let's go over the plan again so everyone is on the same page."

"Wait," I interrupted. "I really want to know what you all were talking about. Grant, you were saying what didn't go together? What did we miss?"

"We were wondering if this same guy could be responsible for all the events we've endured recently," he explained.

"Or is this just another nut job with an axe to grind with Shark," Elijah added.

"Hmmm, that's interesting," I added but thought about it for a few beats. "But don't criminals like that usually get pleasure or whatever by laying claim to things? He hasn't mentioned having a hand in any of the other things, has he? Did I miss that?"

"No, he hasn't. But I think Banks has a point," said Sebastian. "We probably shouldn't discount anything right now. I'll see if I can drag anything out of him after Vela is safe with Elijah."

"You mean safe with me. I'm going," I insisted.

My brother pinched the bridge of his nose in exasperation. "Please don't start again."

"I'm going!" I shouted. His condescending attitude hit me at the wrong angle. "She's my fucking child, and I said I'm going!"

The room fell silent after my outburst, and the men all found other places to look than at me. The only one brave enough to approach me was Jake.

"Star, please." He wrapped his arm around my shoulders and wouldn't let me push away. "Baby, listen to me."

"Jacob, I have to. I have to know I did everything possible. You understand that, don't you?" I could feel the damn tears welling up again.

"I do understand," he said in the gentlest voice. "But do you understand what it would do to me and these other people who care so deeply about you if you were hurt? We couldn't live with that, Cass."

"It's worth the risk," I argued.

"Think about this, then . . . " Elijah put his strong hands on my shoulders and waited for me to meet his gaze. "We need to be one hundred percent focused on Vela and her safe return when we meet with this guy. We don't know how unstable he might be or violent he might get. If you're there too, our focus will be divided, and I think that's a bad idea."

"You have to agree that makes sense, right?" Sebastian asked hopefully.

"Yes, the words make perfect sense." But before they all fully exhaled with relief, I added, "But I'm still going."

"Pia, please."

Leave it to my brother to fight dirty. I knew better than anyone how difficult it was for the man to use that word. Especially while requesting something for personal reasons. But I would not be deterred.

I leveled a final threat that I hoped would shut down this part of the conversation. "I'm going whether you want me there or not. You can loop me in on the plan so it is as safe as possible, or don't. I will be there regardless." Crossing my arms over my chest, I silently challenged any of them to say otherwise.

"Jesus Christ, Cassiopeia," Bas said calmly. "You're going to get yourself—or one of us—killed. Then what? Is all this defiance really worth that to you?"

I was well aware that when he shifted into this deadly calm mode, he was livid. Well, tough shit. This was my daughter's life at stake, and I would not sit back while the men did all the work to bring her home.

"Spare me the melodrama, brother. It's not going to work."

Elijah interrupted our standoff. "We're wasting valuable time here. If you want to go, then fuck it"—he shrugged—"go. But you all need to listen up, because there are a million hidden dangers at the meeting site. I'll go over everything I could identify with the sat cam, but we have to be extra vigilant on the ground. Do you all have your pieces?"

"Pieces?" Jacob repeated and looked a bit pale.

"Guns, junior," Elijah taunted. "I don't suppose you know how to shoot a gun. A real one."

"You don't have to be an asshole. Yes, I know how to shoot a gun. I don't happen to have one on me at the moment, though."

Elijah slid a handgun of some type across my dining room table to my guy, and I felt the room sway.

"Is this necessary?" I screeched. "I don't want more danger for Vela, you guys. You can't go in there like a bunch of outlaws shooting up the place."

"Yes, it's necessary," Elijah answered. "I'm not going to go into an already sketchy situation without as much protection as possible. I won't have any of you do it either. Things are much different for all of us now than they were when we used to do this kind of stupid and dangerous stuff. We all have women and families to think about." Elijah finished his speech and unrolled a large map.

Where the hell did that come from?

And why was that what I was focusing on?

"When should we head out?" I asked. "I would estimate Long Beach is what? Fifty miles south? That's easily ninety minutes of drive time. And that would be with zero traffic on both the 101 and the 405."

"And we all know the likelihood of that," Grant commented.

As usual, Bas had to interject his two cents. "Two hours should be good."

"If we can be on site by eight," Elijah said, "that should give my men enough time to get in place and be ready to engage if necessary."

"No. No engaging," I insisted. "I'm serous, Elijah. I don't want my child in the middle of a street war."

The more I listened to the chatter in the room, the more I pictured my innocent little girl getting caught in the crossfire. My breathing instantly picked up pace, and Jake was on me in a flash.

"All right, darling. Calm down. I see you imagining a thousand horrible scenarios, but you need to stop. We're going to get in and get out. I don't give a shit what the rest of these people want to do while there, but we are getting our daughter and getting to safety as quickly as possible."

Thank every heavenly thing I could name in my semihysterical state for this man. The fact that he knew what was spinning up in my head spoke volumes. We shared such an extensive and complicated history and knew each other so well.

Of course, the other guys and I did too, but they were all so focused on strapping on weapons, communication devices, and other tactical gear, no one noticed the girl in the corner beginning to melt down.

It reminded me of when I was a little girl—probably close to Vela's age, in fact. Bas, Grant, and Elijah were already the best of friends, and I always wanted to tag along on their mischief-making adventures.

My brother would rather drag me along on their missions than leave me in the hands of our drunk father. Oftentimes, I was the lone witness to their troublemaking. But they never could spare time to coddle me. If I went along, I had to keep up, stay quiet, and run like hell if a plan backfired.

This was a far cry from those grade-school adventures, though. My daughter—my reason for living—was at risk. Her very life was in danger, and I had to pull myself together before they made me stay behind.

"Our team is only as strong as its weakest member," Elijah lectured.

Even as teenagers, the guys assumed their natural roles, and he was the tactical guy. Bas was the muscle, and Grant was the con man. Thinking of our youth, even though aspects of it were shitty by anyone's measure, a warm glow filled my body, replacing the anxiety that was trying to take over.

I loved the men in this room for more reasons than I could count, and each so differently, too. But overall, the fact that they had already given up days of their lives to help me get my child back safely raised my level of adoration. Now, even though they had women and children waiting at home for them, they were still rallying around me in my time of need.

I would owe them my life after this. Because Vela *was* my life.

Feeling much better after my anxiety ebbed, I focused on the conversation between the men in the room. A huge map of the Port of Long Beach was laid out on my dining room table, and Elijah drew an invisible line with a capped highlighter.

"This is the way we'll come in." He pointed to an intersection of unmarked roads that appeared to be for equipment traffic rather than personal vehicles.

"Is this area open to the public? Is there the potential for random bystanders to become problematic witnesses?"

My brother's handsome friend shook his head. "No. See this fence and guard shack here?" He pointed first to a fence that surrounded the perimeter of the map and finished on a small gray square that must have been the roof of a security post.

I nodded.

"No one gets past this checkpoint without proper identification, so if anyone is on the piers at this hour, they work there."

Jacob squeezed closer to the table between Grant and me. "Umm, sorry to ask the obvious here, but isn't that going to be an issue? We don't have the"—he made air quotes—"proper identification to be there."

"Oh, junior, you must think you're playing with a bunch of amateurs here," Grant teased and tossed Jacob and me badges with our pictures and basic information. After we stared at them for a few moments, he said, "Your main job is to look and act like you belong there. People only get suspicious when you start acting squirrely."

"Twombley's right," Bas interjected. "When you get onto the property, pretend you're walking in the front door of your own office. Like you do the same thing there every day."

"All right. No problem." I nodded again like the whole thing would be a breeze.

When the men turned back to the map, Jake and I met stares and both bugged our eyes out. We could stress in private while we drove together to Long Beach.

"Okay, kids, pay attention, because we need to shove off in five," Elijah said to call our attention back to the enormous satellite picture.

Thankfully, Jacob rubbed my back in long strokes while we listened to our friend go over the stages of our plan. Having him beside me was the exact grounding I needed to not freak out again. Anytime the words *gun, weapon,* or any form of the word *shoot* were uttered, I could taste stomach bile in the back of my throat.

"How do we know he will even bring her to the meeting?" I asked. "I mean, what if we all show up and it's just this nutcase there by himself?"

"There's no way the guy is going to show up alone," Sebastian replied while staring at me. "He already knows we move in a pack, so he'd be as dumb as he is delusional if he came solo. Dub, listen to me. We're going to get her back. We're not leaving there without her, okay?"

All I could do was nod. The hideous combination of fear and excitement made me feel like I would vomit at any moment.

After swallowing a couple of times, I could finally speak. "I'm going to go tell Wren we're ducking out for some dinner. All of us. Or a few of you are going home to freshen up or whatever." I looked from person to person in the group to make sure that was okay.

"That's a good idea," Elijah said. "Also stress to her that

we need her to stay here in case the asshole calls the house. If she mentions he's only been calling our cell phones, tell her we just don't want to take any chances."

"Got it," I said and started down the hall to the guest room where Wren was napping. The guys' voices faded to a low hum, and I knocked on the door. I tried to focus on my breathing, or I'd give myself away. I was a terrible liar, and everyone knew it. Hopefully, she wouldn't give me too much of a hassle. She definitely wasn't coming with us. I would flat-out refuse.

"Hey, beautiful, you up?" I whispered into the dark room. With a small exhale of relief, I counted the lack of light a plus in my favor.

Her groggy voice came from the mountain of pillows and blankets. As long as I'd known the young woman, she'd wrapped herself in the bed clothes like a mummy when she slept. Something about feeling safer and more secure so she could relax enough to bring on zees.

"Yeah. Hey." There was a lot of shuffling around, and then I could hear her more clearly. "What's going on?" Suddenly, she sprang to a sitting position and asked, "Is she back? Did you find her?"

Now that my eyes had adjusted more to the scant amount of light coming in from the hallway, it was enough to see her silhouette.

My assistant attempted to smooth down her messy hair and said, "I am so sorry I fell asleep. Of all the times to be exhausted. Please forgive me. I feel like such a shit."

"Don't be ridiculous," I said while searching where I estimated her hands would be and finally held them in my own. I gave her a gentle squeeze and assured her, "Baby, it's fine. Not much can be done until we hear from the guy again anyway. In fact, that's why I came in here."

Shit. Here goes nothing.

I continued explaining, using the story line we'd agreed upon in the dining room. I gave her the portable handset from the house phone to keep beside her in bed, and by the time I was ready to walk out of the room, she was lying down again and apparently too tired to argue any point she might have questioned.

"Why don't you just sleep here tonight? That way you don't have to be disturbed again until morning," I reasoned with her. Even then, all I heard was a muffled version of *okay*.

That seemed too easy. But, instead of pressing my luck, I chalked it up to how exhausted she was. She'd probably agree to anything at that moment just so I would let her get back to sleeping.

When I emerged from the guest room, Jacob was leaning against the opposite wall of the hallway.

"How did it go?" he asked and offered his open arms for me to cuddle into.

This was getting to be a bad habit. I liked the comfort and courage I found in his embrace a little too much for my own good. If he eventually decided my life was too chaotic and too dangerous to be a part of, how would I get along without him? If I continued to allow myself to be mentally and emotionally vulnerable when he was around, I'd be devastated if he left.

"I think she was already sleeping before I left the room. The poor thing is so wiped out." I couldn't help but nuzzle my nose into his neck because he smelled divine. My shoulders dropped in increments as I relaxed in his arms.

But then one of the guys' voices traveled down the hallway. "Let's move out, people." They all had such deep, resonant voices, when they raised their volume, it was harder to determine the speaker.

Jacob pulled back to look down at me. "You ready to do this?"

I gave one quick nod because I couldn't trust my voice to sound confident.

He studied me a beat too long, and my defenses rose. "Star," he sighed. "No one will be upset if you hold the fort here. Probably happier about it, really. I know it's increasing your anxiety."

"And you're just cool as a cucumber?" I assessed him skeptically.

"No, I'm not," he huffed. "Quite the opposite, actually. So, I can imagine what's going on in here." He put his strong hand over my heart, and surely he felt how the thing was keeping a techno beat.

I broke away from our embrace. "Let's just go get our girl. My nerves aren't going to settle down until my child is safe and back in this house."

"Agreed. Let's do this."

Traffic was as expected, but we all arrived at the agreed upon parking area near Pier J at the Port of Long Beach with plenty of time. The side streets in the surrounding area were quiet at that hour, so we were able to park close to each other and not in a public pay lot. Elijah pointed out that those lots are always under significant security camera coverage, and we definitely didn't want to be identified on the scene in case something went sideways.

I was so glad these men had their act together, because I could barely walk and talk at the same time currently. Jake and I held hands and strode across the street to meet up with the guys.

"Okay, everyone has their IDs?" Elijah asked.

We all nodded, and I gave my pocket a quick feel to make sure it was still in there. Christ, this was such a sketchy plan. If we were stopped by pier security and were asked a bunch of questions, I wasn't confident I'd be able to fool them. I stuck closer to Jake just to feel the warmth of his body and ground myself before I spun up with panic.

We looked ridiculous, too. We were all dressed in black with black ball caps pulled down low over our eyes. We looked more like Janet Jackson's Rhythm Nation backup dancers than regular citizens trying to rescue a child.

"I'm freaking out, you guys," I admitted, and at least two heads swung my way.

"Pia, pull it together," my brother growled. "Let's go get our girl and get out of here. That's all that's going to happen. You can't *act* suspicious, or someone will *get* suspicious. We went over this."

He was losing the small amount of patience he normally possessed, and his lecture wasn't helping my nerves in the least. Thankfully, Jake wrapped a reassuring arm around my shoulders and held me against his body while we continued walking. The men had such long strides, I felt like I had to jog to keep pace.

By some stroke of luck, when we got to the guard shack at the head of the pier, no one was inside. We didn't bother standing around to debate where the man might be. We just kept walking. I didn't think I breathed at all until we were twenty-five yards down the bike path. I sent out a silent prayer to the universe that things continued to go as smoothly.

A girl can dream, right?

CHAPTER TWELVE

JACOB

After walking briskly for about ten minutes, we rounded the last bend of the bike trail. Here, the plan was to split up and stay out of sight. Well, everyone but Sebastian and Pia, since that's who the guy insisted show up.

My stomach was in knots sending her down the rest of the path without me. I couldn't bear to have something happen to her. To either of my girls.

Grant and I were paired together for this portion of the operation, and trying to find a suitable place the dude could hide was our biggest challenge so far. At his height, it wasn't as easy to duck under or slide behind something. Across the path I spotted three full bushes and nudged his shoulder to catch his attention. I motioned to the potential hiding spot, and he gave a quick nod.

Once we were hidden, I peeked down the bike path to keep my eye on Pia. She and Sebastian stood in the middle of the wide sidewalk facing opposite directions so they wouldn't be caught off guard no matter which way the guy approached from.

I readjusted my earpiece when I heard a bunch of static. What the hell was going on with this thing? Grant had his eyes on me, and I pointed to the damn device crackling in my ear canal. The tall man gave a quick nod. Hopefully, he meant an affirmative answer to the question I couldn't outright ask. *Are you hearing that?*

Sebastian and Pia's conversation began flowing from the static. It was like we were standing right there with them, even though they had to be fifty yards away.

"Everyone's hot. Just so you know. This way, if you need help, we will all hear it immediately," Elijah explained.

From the plans we reviewed at the house, he should be up the trail in the opposite direction of Grant and me. I definitely couldn't see him from my spot in the bushes, and the night looked to be getting darker with each passing minute.

Sebastian mumbled, "Inbound. I think this is our guy."

Pia began to panic immediately. "Where is Vela? Why isn't she with him?"

My natural instinct was to calm her. "Star, breathe. Maybe that's not him. Stay calm and let's see how this plays out."

I saw her dip her head a couple times while she listened to my comforting words.

"This guy look familiar to anyone?" Bas grumbled. "Twombley?"

"Can't tell yet. It's dark as shit down there from the view junior and I have," he replied, and I wanted to elbow the guy in the stomach. That nickname was wearing on my already-thin nerves.

Elijah's voice came through the device, "Can you two move closer to one of the lights? It's really hard to see you from my spot too."

The siblings started toward the stranger until Elijah confirmed the lighting was better for all of us. At the same time the man continued to approach until he was about twenty-five feet from the Sharks.

He had both hands in the front pockets of a black hooded sweatshirt, and my pulse spiked. Christ, what if he had a weapon? His hood was up and pulled down as far as the fabric would stretch to obscure his face. Definitely couldn't tell his hair color or even if he had facial hair from where we hid in the bushes. Fucker thought this meeting through, for sure. Any of us would be hard pressed to identify the guy.

"Isn't this a quaint family reunion?" he finally said.

"Yes, but there's an obvious absentee," Bas said casually.

"Where's my daughter?" Pia shouted, and the bastard grinned so wide I could count his teeth from my hiding spot.

"Chill, Dub," Sebastian muttered to his sister.

"She's close by. Don't worry your pretty head, sister," the creep hissed.

"What do you want?" Sebastian confronted the man squarely. "You wanted us here." He spread his arms wide. "Here we are."

"Now, now, what's the rush? I've waited twenty-seven years to come face-to-face with the pair of you." The stranger made a sweeping gesture in front of the siblings. "Let me drink you in."

"Stop fucking around. Tell me what you want and let the child go."

"Well, you see, brother, there's a bit of a score to settle between the three of us. While the two of you have been living like royalty, I've been living in the tent city under the 10 freeway. I mean, I'd have you over for tea and finger sandwiches, but the neighbors aren't super friendly, you know?"

"Oh my God," Pia gasped and covered her mouth with trembling fingers. "That's where you've had my child?"

"Don't get high and mighty with me, lady," he said and

then chuckled. The unpleasant sound turned into a cackle. The dude was definitely skirting the edge of sanity.

"Look. I'm only going to stand here for so long and entertain your bullshit," Bas threatened. "Either tell me what you want and hand over my niece, or go fuck yourself."

"Take it easy, Shark," Elijah said into his mic. "Tell him to show his hands."

Sebastian's demeanor shifted slightly. He still wouldn't submit an inch of control in the situation, but his tone was less Pitbull and more German Shepherd. "Let's see your hands, asshole. We're not looking for unnecessary attention from LAPD, and I doubt you are either. Bloodshed will obtain exactly that."

"Ummm—no. See, here's the thing. You're used to getting your way. I get that. You're used to being the one who calls all the shots. Get that too. But things are about to change. I'm in control of this situation, and you'll do what I say. Not the other way around." The guy smiled smugly.

Bas groaned. "Super."

"Sebastian," Pia muttered through what sounded like clenched teeth. "Just do what he wants. We have to get Vela."

"Ahhh, see? I always suspected our sister was the brains in the family."

"Listen, buddy," Bas started while pinching the bridge of his nose. "We all know you're not our dead brother. Just cut the bullshit. It's disrespectful to the lost life of an infant who never stood a chance. It's so unnecessary."

"Where's my daughter?" Pia demanded.

The lunatic started pacing circles around the siblings. "See, that's where you're wrong, dearest brother. I know you were told your mother and brother died within hours of each other, but that's not really how it all went down."

"Okay," Bas said in a very patronizing manner. "Tell us what happened, then." It was difficult to tell from our vantage point in the bushes, but I was pretty sure his comment was accompanied by an eye roll too.

"You see, it just so happened there was a nurse working the night I was born. The woman wasn't stable and should never have been working around infants." Then the guy muttered, "Shouldn't have been near kids of any age, really." He seemed to drift into a memory and stood staring for a few beats.

Bas took a step toward the guy, and everyone in our group held his breath. *What the hell was he doing?* "Is there a point to this story, or are you just going to stand there daydreaming?"

The comment shook the guy from his stall, so with a quick twist of his head, he continued. "Later in my childhood, my mother, as I thought she was, told me she swapped me with another infant who was indeed dead and told the Sharks that I had passed. Apparently, our mother was in distress during the later stages of labor and delivery, so it was easy to confuse her with details. From what I've gathered, dear old Dad was a bit of a drinker, so he wasn't in a clear state of mind either. No one questioned my new mother about the details."

Not a word was uttered after that bomb dropped. Could this nutcase actually be a Shark?

"Why are you coming around now? It's been, what? Twenty-some years?" Shark shook his head, trying to make sense of the guy's tale. "Why wait so long? And why not just come forward? Why involve another innocent child?"

"Hey now, let's not leave out all the other fun I've been having at your expense. The shark in your backyard was priceless. You have to admit that at least." The guy had a wide smile while he waited for his siblings' praise.

"Dude, you're seriously fucked in the head," Bas replied instead of giving the psycho the props he was looking for.

But every time he insulted the guy, it clicked up the man's temper by a subtle degree. Sebastian was being way too confrontational for my liking. It was my kid's life on the line here. How dare he be so cavalier.

"Shark, tone down the insults, man. Until we get Vela," I whispered over coms. I watched Pia tense even more after my comment and felt like shit that I added to her fear. But someone needed to keep Sebastian grounded.

"If I were you, I wouldn't be so mouthy to the man who has the power in this situation," the man threatened.

Bas simply shrugged. Fucking shrugged!

So the man raised his voice to deliver his next bit of information. "Maybe your friend Grant Twombley will vouch for me when he's reminded of the nine days we spent together at sea, hmmm?" The stranger let his comment hang in the cooling night air. Then followed with, "I can only assume you have backup here?"

With that comment, Grant stiffened. "Motherfucker. What is this guy playing at?"

"I don't know, man, but take the com device out if he has any verbal ammunition that can fuck with you," I advised the tall man. "You don't need to hear his bullshit."

I only knew the sparse details Pia had filled in for me regarding Grant's abduction, and she was pretty sure she only had the basics herself. In the past, I'd witnessed Grant completely metamorphosize into a zombie after being triggered by some random noise, comment, or smell.

We needed every member of our team functioning at peak performance, so Twombley had to do what he could to block this asshole out of his head.

Grant followed my advice and yanked the earpiece out. But it may have been too late. Already, his breathing accelerated, and where he was calm and still before, he was now shifty and restless.

"Okay, big guy," I said as quietly and soothingly as possible. I reached out to put a reassuring palm on his shoulder but thought better of it and drew back. "Watch me for cues that we're moving or whatever."

He nodded, and I thought that was a good sign. He was still listening and processing in the present.

Out on the bike path, the standoff continued. The three people were locked in an intense stare-down after the creep took that shot at Grant. The Sharks were fiercely loyal to their friends, and I was really surprised Bas had resisted hitting the dude at that point.

"Okay, okay. Let's stop this nonsense," Pia said in a steady and sure voice.

That's my girl.

"Let's say we believe your story and you really are Caleb Shark," she continued, "our brother who we thought died at birth."

Bas interrupted, "Yes. Let's play make believe, and let's all pretend you are back from the dead."

"Sebastian," Pia pleaded with her brother. "Stop."

To the stranger she said, "What comes next in your grand plan? We agree you are who you say you are. Then what? Where do we go from here?"

I wanted to rush out onto that path and wrap her in the safest, most loving embrace. She was being so brave and smart.

"Yes—bruhhh-therrrr. Where do you see this going? A

new place setting at the holiday table? A stocking with your name embroidered on the top to hang on the mantel? Shit, man"—Bas threw his arms out wide—"tell us and it's yours."

Why couldn't he keep his damn mouth shut? Pia had done a great job moving the whole thing forward, but with Sebastian antagonizing the crazy fool each time he spoke, I thought maybe the tycoon had a death wish.

"You should be taking this more seriously, Sebastian," the man threatened. "I would've thought from all the times I watched you that your niece meant more to you than that."

"If you had an ounce of Shark blood in your veins, you would never harm a child," Sebastian challenged. "After all we went through when we were children, that's the last thing any of us would do."

I didn't know if he was trying reverse psychology on the guy, or if this whole plan had gone tits up and we were all flying by the seats of our pants.

"Ah, speaking of Shark blood," the stranger said with renewed enthusiasm, "I brought you something." Finally, he took his hands from his pockets, and everyone froze.

In one hand, he held what looked like a vial of blood. The glass tube even had a purple rubber top like I'd seen many times while having blood drawn.

"This sample was drawn from my arm before we came here. Do whatever you want with it to prove I am who I say I am. DNA doesn't lie." He tossed the vial in Sebastian's direction with no warning.

Luckily, the boss man was agile and alert, so he caught the thing before it smashed on the ground. I watched Pia's face as it twisted with horror before her brother made the catch.

"This is the last time I'm going to ask you, asshole. What

do you want from us? Why abduct and terrify a child if you just want to grandstand for attention?"

"Because I know she's a valuable asset to everyone in this group. I knew she would be the ultimate ace in my hand. First, when we took your tall friend, I thought that would bring you out of your castle in the clouds." He shook his head and looked disappointed. "But all that did was send his little hottie closer to the edge of insanity and cause a lot of problems for my business."

"Your business? What is that, exactly?"

"Aww, come on, you already know. Your bestie got a good long look up close and personal with my operation."

"Stop speaking in fucking riddles and get to the point," Bas barked.

The creep gave a careless shrug. "I followed in my big brother's footsteps. I mean, when I saw how much money you were making moving freight, I figured I'd give it a shot. I just deal in a different type of . . . cargo."

"What you're doing is nothing like what I do. Dumping human bodies at sea is illegal." Bas shook his head. "You're nothing like me."

Holy. Shit. I knew these guys were messing with some lowlifes, but I had no idea how low. My anxiety swelled knowing a man capable of this type of activity had my daughter.

Out of instinct and a healthy amount of panic, I surged forward to attack the guy.

But Twombley threw his body on top of mine to keep me in our hiding spot, but surely we just gave up our location with the commotion.

"What the fuck are you doing?" Grant hissed in a furious whisper.

"That scumbag has my kid," I growled back. "This bullshit has to end right now."

"You'll fuck up the whole plan if you charge out there. Get a grip, man."

Elijah's furious voice came in my ear. "What are you two doing? Square dancing?"

"I've heard all I can take. Why is he toying with the guy so much? We were supposed to get our daughter and get the fuck out of here," I explained in a rush.

"Do you see her here, junior?"

"Stop fucking calling me that. And no…I don't." Goddammit, he was right. But I could jump the guy and demand he tell me where she was.

"Settle the fuck down and wait. My men are searching the area, trying to see how many backups this guy has and if Vela is even here. But if you pull another stunt like that, he'll run."

Grant had his earpiece back in, so he heard his buddy's warning. He nodded along as Banks spoke, and I gave him a quick once-over, trying to decide if I could take him on and clear my way.

"Whatever idea you're cooking up right now"—the guy actually poked me right in the center of my forehead—"knock it the fuck off."

I swung wildly to push his hand away, but it was already back at his side. The guy moved quickly for someone his height—stealthy too.

My woman must've reached her limit then too. She said to her brother, "Bas, let's get out of here. If he isn't going to return my daughter, why entertain this gibberish?"

"Now, now. Patience truly is a virtue. I have some friends coming down the bike trail with her right now. That only gives the three of us a few more minutes of alone time."

"Oh, fucking joy," Sebastian grumbled.

Something in the guy snapped from Sebastian's comment, and he launched himself at Shark and gripped both halves of his jacket. The two men were face to face, and even from my obstructed and distant vantage point, you could see the family resemblance.

Could this guy really be telling the truth?

CHAPTER THIRTEEN

PIA

"Get your fucking hands off me, loser." My brother violently threw his arms out and pushed the creepy guy away. When he regained space between the man and himself, he straightened his coat with a mighty scowl. "Unless you want to pick your teeth up off the ground along with your self-respect, I suggest you keep your hands to yourself, asshole."

Then, Bas turned to me and said, "Yeah, let's get out of here. I've heard about all I can take for tonight."

Even though I was the one who offered the suggestion in the first place, panic overcame me. We had endured all this man's crazy dramatics, and I wasn't two inches closer to getting my child back in my arms.

A rumbling sound came from behind us on the bike path. It sounded like a grocery cart being wheeled over uneven pavement, and Bas shifted his eyes past me in that direction. Foolishly, I turned my entire body. Of course, showing my back to the unstable third member of our conversation was dumb on so many levels, but I was transfixed with what I saw.

And then completely horrified.

A large, burly, and unkempt man was wheeling a flatbed trolly down the path. On the flat surface of the cart was what looked like a large-breed dog crate. It didn't take the man long to get close enough to see my daughter was shoved inside. Her big, terrified, tear-filled eyes shined in the lights that illuminated the trail.

"Oh my God! Oh my God," I repeated and started toward her, only to instantly be yanked back by a firm hand on my shoulder. I turned to see Sebastian giving me a slight head shake.

Was he insane? I couldn't stand here a minute longer and bear witness to my child being treated like an animal.

"What?" I growled. "I need to... She needs me... Bas." I started the statement strong and angry and ended it with a pleading whimper.

"Just wait, Dub," he said for only my ears. "Let's make sure it's safe. For her *and* for you." And it was a strong tactic. Pointing out her potential danger because of my actions was the quickest way to freeze me in my tracks. I whirled back to Caleb—if he was indeed who he said he was—and demanded answers.

"Tell me what you want. Anything. Anything at all, and it's yours. Just let me get her out of there."

"Mama?" Vela's voice was a shadow of what it normally was, and it cracked me wide open.

"Please. Whatever I'm capable of giving you," I said again.

"No, dear sister. It's not you I need promises from. It's our brother here"—he lifted his chin toward Sebastian—"who will give in to my demands. Hell, I may even record it for posterity."

"You've gone too far, freak." Bas glared at the guy with a look so intense even I sucked in a breath. "You'll pay for this." Seeing his niece in a fucking dog cage was making my brother tremble with rage.

Just as I registered the lethal amount of anger rolling off

Bas, he lunged toward Caleb and tackled him to the ground in a move worthy of a Monday Night Football highlight reel. After one shoulder check to the stomach, both men dropped to the ground.

Caleb hit the sidewalk first with a dense thud. His head flew back from the momentum of their combined bodies and smacked the concrete. The noise was sickening and satisfying at the same time.

Sebastian wrapped his meaty hand around the other man's neck and leveraged his body weight into the choke hold. His opponent went from beet red to purple in seconds.

"Sebastian, you're going to kill him!" I shouted and looked frantically to the spots I knew the others were concealed. "Do something!" I yelled into the night sky, and feet pounding on the sidewalk made me swing around in the opposite direction to see my daughter still in the crate. The retreating shadows of at least two people faded into the night scenery.

Elijah gave up the safety of his hiding spot to help Sebastian, so I ran toward Vela as she cried out again.

"Mama, please help me!"

The man who was wheeling the cart stepped between my child and me, inciting a warning growl from the depths of my soul. While he was distracted with me, Grant and Jacob came up from behind with their fingers pressed to their lips, warning me to stay quiet about their arrival.

There was no way to know what they had planned, so I dug deep for courage and poured on the emotions to keep the man distracted.

"Please. Please, I'm begging you. Let her out of there. I'll give you whatever you want." It didn't take a lot of acting skill to produce tears in the tense situation, but the big guy had other ideas about my method of payment.

Judging by the salacious gleam in his eye, he wasn't thinking about Venmo. When his wide grin made my entire body skitter with disgust, I saw he was missing several front teeth.

This was probably one of the men who held Grant captive. And probably part of the gang that attacked Hannah at the Edge jobsite, too.

Grant must have recognized the guy at first sight, because he led the advance from behind. I watched in frozen horror as he lifted a huge rock above his head and smashed the guy in the back of the skull with it. The creep crumbled to the ground, and blood immediately pooled around his head. I got one glance of his lifeless eyes before I rushed to Vela's aid.

"Star, baby," I gasped and frantically worked at the mechanism on the cage. "You okay? I'm going to get you out of there. Hold on."

My daughter came unglued and thrashed inside the carrier with the same level of panic I felt. Trying her best to get the front door open, she yanked and pushed on the metal grate.

"Vela!" I shouted through my tears as she freaked out, making the entire crate rock and sway. It was impossible to unlatch the clasp while she was making the whole thing quake.

"Get me out! Get me out! Mama! Help me!"

We were both yelling our own demands until one very stern voice froze us both.

"Girls!" It was Jacob, and our child stilled at once. "Darling, be still so we can work this latch open." When she was motionless for more than a moment, he added, "Thank you for listening."

"I'm so scared, Papa. Help me, please," she whimpered,

and if any part of my heart were still intact, that shattered it.

I stood by and watched Jacob finally get the cage open and pull her into his arms. He crumbled to the pavement while cradling her, and I threw myself into them.

"Thank God! Thank God," I wailed and gripped on to Jacob's arm. "Thank you!"

"Let's get the hell out of here," he said to me over our daughter's head.

I was already nodding before he finished his thought but then scanned the area for a direction to bolt and saw the aftermath of the altercation. Jake followed my gaze, where it stalled on the dead man lying in a river of black blood, and immediately stepped in my line of sight.

"Let's go the other way," he said, but I was torn. I couldn't leave my brother and friends here in danger, but I wanted to run as fast as my legs would carry me and never look back.

"Go, Dub! Get the hell out of here!" my brother barked, and that was all I needed to hear to get my feet moving. "We'll meet back at your house."

I had no idea how long that damn bike path was, but it was definitely farther than I had run in years. Thank God Jake carried our daughter the entire way, because I never would've made it.

When we got to my SUV, I couldn't bring myself to leave her in the back seat alone. I caught my guy's attention and said, "Can you drive? I'll sit in back."

"Good call," he replied and opened the door with his free hand and shoved our child into my arms once I was inside.

She felt so small and fragile, and her expressionless face freaked me out. There was a good chance she was in shock, so I stopped Jake from getting behind the wheel with a request.

"Can you go in the hatch and grab the blanket I have back there? I think she's cold."

Without a word, he hustled around to the rear of the vehicle, and I listened as he popped the back door open and shuffled around for the blanket I always had on standby. Years of park playdates, soccer games, and beach outings taught me that valuable lesson.

"There's an emergency pack in the same spot. Can you toss it to me?" I asked and stroked Vela's hair away from her face.

"Star?" I asked in the gentlest voice I had. "Baby, are you hungry? I have juice boxes." I said it as a question to try to coax a response from her. But she just stared past me to the opposite side of the car.

"This it?" Jacob asked, sounding a bit bewildered.

I looked over my shoulder and saw the red insulated lunch bag I kept for blood sugar emergencies or small child hangry moments. My daughter was much like her uncle Grant when she didn't have food every few hours. She became a very testy version of herself and was most unpleasant to deal with.

My God, what I wouldn't give to hear her throw a fit right now.

After closing the hatch, her father was back around to our side of the car and leaned in to tuck the blanket around us both.

"Do you have your seat belt on under there? Should I secure it around you both?"

"Good idea," I said and released the two halves so he could do it his way.

The automatic retraction of the belt snapped the thing out of his hand, and he muttered some choice words under his breath.

He shot his stare to mine and mouthed *sorry* when he realized he had just turned the interior of my car blue with all the profanity.

We both seemed to conclude it was the least of our problems.

Vela still hadn't said a word, and her little body's trembling seemed to be worse.

"Take us home, please," I said to Jacob. I never wanted to see the Port of Long Beach again. Hell, I'd avoid the entire city just so I didn't have to be triggered by the memory of what happened here.

"Jake!" That time I put some force into the volume of my voice, and he jumped like I just popped out from the bushes to startle him. "Are you sure you're okay to drive?"

"Yeah, I'm good," he tried to reassure me, but I could see the way his eyes were narrowed and his lips were pressed tightly.

I thought we'd both aged eight years in one night. He looked as shitty as I felt.

We sped home in very light traffic. It was a small victory I would gladly take. It would've been the last straw of my composure if we had to endure LA traffic after all we'd been through. The same trek that earlier took more than two hours was done in about forty-five minutes.

But they were still some of the longest minutes I could remember. My daughter was close to catatonic, and no matter what I asked or offered, she didn't respond. Hell, I wasn't sure she even blinked her eyes for the better part of an hour. I reminded myself over and over to be patient with her. She had been through a terrible ordeal, and I was sure there would be scars for years to come.

With lips pressed to the top of her head, I quietly said, "We're home, baby."

"Mama?" she finally spoke, but her normally sweet, melodic voice was raspy and dry.

"What is it, Star?"

"Will I have to go back there? To my uncle's house?" Her eyes were wide and frightened, and the pain in my chest prevented me from speaking.

Jacob was standing at the open car door waiting to take her from my arms. When he saw the amount of emotion clogging my throat, he answered instead.

"No, baby. Never again. If I have any say in the matter." He paused and then repeated, "Never again."

She studied him carefully. What else was this feeling displayed on her face? Distrust? Doubt? I couldn't tell exactly.

Finally, she gave her head a slow dip and said, "Okay. Good. I didn't like that visit at all. It was the worst sleepover ever."

I held her against my chest a little longer. Jacob gave us all the time we needed and kept a supportive hand spread across my back. Just that little reassuring touch gave me the courage I needed to ask her some really tough questions.

"Vela?"

"Yes, ma'am?"

I screwed up my face with her response. She'd never addressed me that way, and it gave me chills hearing it now. That term of respect dragged me back to an incident with my father that I couldn't quite pluck out of my memory. I just remembered how terrifying it had been when that man was angry.

There was no room in my heart or my head for shitty

memories, though. But I couldn't help thinking about my father after possibly meeting my younger brother. What was his childhood like? Did he grow up in a loving home? Judging by his bitterness, it wasn't likely.

Not as though Bas and I had a great time either. But instead of feeling sad for the man, I felt so confused from the scene at the pier. I tried to pull details from the night that would prove the guy was a scam artist. Because as terrible as it sounded, I really didn't need another complication in my life. And really, finding out Caleb was actually alive all these years would give birth to a whole hornet's nest of issues.

Too lost in my own thoughts, I forgot I had initiated a conversation with Vela and we were all huddled in and around the back passenger side of the car. Maybe moving inside would be better. But the fact that she snapped out of the daze she had been in and answered me was encouraging. For the moment at least.

"Listen to me, Star. We don't have to talk about it right now, okay?" I waited for her to give me some sort of sign she was absorbing my words.

Her hollow eyes were trained right on me.

Choosing my words very carefully, I asked her the question that stood out from the others. God, I was so worried about causing more harm because I selfishly needed to close some of the open doors in my mind. Would mentioning her kidnapper bring on more trauma than the explanation of how this all happened was worth?

"When you're ready, I'd like you to tell me what happened. How did you leave school with that man? Or maybe, *why* did you do that? Have you ever met him before?"

She stared at me for an eternity, and I was just about to urge her into Jake's arms, when she nodded once.

"You'd met him before? Where?" My voice pitched high with disbelief. How I prayed she was mistaken.

My talking machine of a child continued the vacant gaze for long moments, so Jacob interjected.

"Sweetheart, are you tired? Or hungry?" He hadn't spent much time with her up to that point, but from the looks he kept sneaking to me above her head, he definitely knew she was way off her normal mien.

But instead of a helpful answer, my daughter just shrugged.

Shrugged?

I could probably count the number of times on my thumbs that my opinionated little queen shrugged in her entire life.

"Let's go inside. If you think of something that sounds good to eat, I'll gladly fix it for you. I know Wren is very anxious to see you home safely too."

When Jacob reached for Vela, she skittered back from him and burrowed her face into my neck. He and I met confused stares, but he took her cue and dropped his arms. I didn't miss the look of hurt that flashed across his face, but it was gone as quickly as it came. We all had to just give her the space she needed and let her readjust to us.

So help me...if it came to light that the man calling himself Caleb touched my child in the slightest inappropriate way, I would ensure he stopped breathing for real this time.

CHAPTER FOURTEEN

JACOB

Well, I'd be lying if I said her rejection didn't sting a bit. Okay, a lot. But one look at her exhausted little face and disheveled clothes and hair, and I pulled up my own nonsense and focused back on Vela. My feelings weren't the important thing in this mess. They didn't even merit another second of brain time.

Inside the house, Wren was waiting to greet us. We weren't sure if she would be sleeping or not, so Pia decided not to text her with the news that we got our child back safely.

The young woman charged our sluggish group as we moved deeper into the house and attempted to take Vela from her boss but got a similar reaction as the one I received moments ago.

Wren searched Pia's watchful gaze, and I saw the women exchange a quick wordless conversation. Their deep connection was apparent when Wren gave a nod and backed away by a few steps.

"Star? Do you want to take a bath?" Wren asked. "Or a shower maybe?"

"No, thank you, ma'am," she croaked from the safety of her mother's neck.

This level of deference was unusual, and I noticed it in the car as well. Again, the women exchanged a quick look, but this time, no one had the answer to what the hell was going on in the child's mind.

Silently I swore to exact some meaningful retribution on my newly discovered brother-in-law to be. Whatever the man was foolish enough to have done to our child, he would pay dearly for it. I'd see to it personally.

"What if I help?" Pia offered our little one.

"No thank you. I can do it myself," she replied and squirmed enough to finally be set on her own feet.

"Okay. Why don't I fix some mac and cheese while you get cleaned up? Or I can order a pizza?" Pia was trying all her favorites to coax her out of this unfamiliar mood.

"No, thank you," she nearly whispered and trudged down the hallway.

We all stood motionless while following her progress with focused ears as she went into her room and quietly closed the door.

Pia sank onto one of the stools at the island and buried her face in her hands. Wren and I must have had the same goal in mind when we converged on her from either side.

Comfort her. Somehow make this nightmare disappear.

"Star," I said with all the love and tenderness I felt inside. I wanted to shield her from any sort of pain for the rest of our lives. Our daughter, too. And I realized I'd come off the blocks as an epic failure. Internally, I vowed to spend every day moving forward making that up to her. To them.

"I'm fine," she said angrily but didn't drop her hands.

I sent Wren a pleading stare, and the woman was so in tune with the emotions that she gave me a quick nod and bustled off toward Vela's room.

Pulling my woman's hands down, I saw the proof of just how fine she wasn't.

"Tell me how to help you, darling. Let me carry the burden for you or, at the very least, beside you."

Tear after tear continued to stream down her pink cheeks, and each one felt like a tiny dagger being driven into my heart.

"Seriously, Jacob. I'm okay. If I don't let this out, though, things will get ugly. I'm sorry you've had to watch me cry so often in the short amount of time you've been back in my life."

"Please don't apologize to me for showing emotions. Don't be ridiculous. You know"—I tried to go for a lighter tone, but I wasn't sure I pulled it off—"it's not a crime or a character flaw to let someone help you."

She gave me a slight head tilt and the very slightest shadow of a smile. "I know that. But please be patient and remember I've been doing this alone for close to nine years. It's not in my general nature to seek out help."

"Let me ask you this, then," I proposed. "Would you accept someone's help if it wasn't to benefit just you but also our child?" This seemed like a vital question for our future. It also seemed like I was asking her a question I already knew the answer to.

When we were in college, she was one of the most altruistic humans I'd ever met. If something had caused that spirit to be diminished, it would be a true loss for the people around her. Dare I say for the world at large, too. It would be a hard fact to reconcile for me specifically since it was one of the most beautiful parts of her. One of the thousands of things I loved about her.

Either she was too tired to entertain my question, or I'd offended her by asking it. Pia stared at me for a long moment, not saying anything.

Normally, I could see a particular light in her blue eyes

that I always imagined were new ideas and provocative thoughts bouncing around her busy mind. But now, her stare was almost vacant.

Then it hit me, and I already knew I was about to piss her off even more.

"Babe, have you checked your sugar lately?"

"No. I've been a little busy, you know?" she whipped back with a heavy dose of attitude.

I leaned closer to her in case our daughter was about to pull one of her little appearing acts. Always at the most inopportune time, I might add.

"Excuse me, Ms. Shark," I warned. "Is that attitude just for me, or will everyone be getting a sample?"

She continued to glare, and I expected to see burn marks alongside the pollen and dried mud on my filthy shirt. I wondered if she knew the effect her insolent stare had on my body. And if she knew, was that the path she wanted to wander down after having one of the most trying days of our lives? I certainly wouldn't turn her away. In fact, a long hard fuck would probably do us both some good.

Until we had some privacy, I would care for her in the other ways I knew.

"Where's your supply kit? I'll get it for you," I offered, but she shot to her feet.

What the hell is going on?

When her next comment had the exact same tone Vela's had regarding her bath, I had a better understanding. My girls were fiercely independent. Having been thrust into a situation that tested their ability to handle themselves, they battled back with an overdose of independence.

"I can do it," she muttered and zombie-shuffled from the room.

My guess was that they both felt like they had failed when tested. Now, they would come back swinging twice as hard to prove to those around them that they really were capable of doing everything for themselves.

I felt supremely aggravated with society and possibly the male gender for fucking up women's heads this way. How did it become wrong to need or accept help now and then? Especially when in crisis?

My phone signaled an incoming text that I was unexpectedly glad to read. The guys were all heading to their own homes for the night after I reassured Shark his niece was okay. We agreed to talk sometime the next day.

A few minutes passed and Pia hadn't returned to the kitchen, so I went looking for her. I found her in her ensuite bathroom leaning over the sink. Her testing supplies were strewn across the counter like she turned the little bag upside down and let everything scatter.

Pia leaned forward on braced arms and hung her head low between them. Her whole body was tense and shaking, and I rushed to her side.

"Hey, hey. What's going on, Star?" I said as calmly as possible.

She wouldn't look at me, so I gripped her shoulders and turned her to face me.

She was crying again, and this time she really lost it.

Following instinct, I bent low and scooped her into my arms. Of course, she protested the whole time.

"Jake, stop."

"No, darling. You stop. Stop this stubbornness and let me help you." I deposited her on the bed, and she immediately turned onto her side, facing away from me. That was fine. I just went to the other side. I passed along the information about her brother and his two sidekicks while I climbed onto the mattress and gathered her in my arms.

"Now tell me what's going on," I insisted.

No response.

"Pia, talk to me."

"I'm just exhausted. And so damn emotional. It just keeps hitting me like a sucker punch." She sniffed and tried to regain her composure. But I'd have none of that.

"There's nothing wrong with crying. Clearly your body needs it right now, so just do it. Let it out. Hopefully, once you get through it, you'll feel a little bit more like yourself. More in control."

I said that last sentence and immediately thought it would be the next thing she gave me attitude about. She was going to end up with a good old-fashioned spanking if she didn't chill out. Instead, she wrapped her arms around my neck and pulled me closer. The embrace was very intimate, and I had to silently warn my dick to behave. The last thing I needed right now was a hard-on.

"There you go," I crooned beside her ear while reciprocating the tight hug. Hopefully, she would let me care for her—at least right now.

I hooked my toes into the throw blanket that was artfully arranged at the base of the bed and dragged it closer to grab with my hand. As I spread it over her back and shoulders, she finally met my gaze.

And nearly broke me.

"Baby, what's going on? I understand you've had some very trying days. This seems like something else, though. Am I reading you right?"

If she said she was fine, I vowed to punish her for so blatantly lying. Maybe if I asked questions, it would be easier for her to identify what had her so upset.

"I— I don't understand it myself," she stammered, and the frustration released a fresh wave of tears.

"Okay, darling," I said and planted a kiss on the top of her head. "Did you test your sugar, or were you in the process of that when I walked in?" I was careful to modulate my voice so it didn't come out sounding accusatory or belittling.

Pia gave her head a short shake and explained, "No. I dropped my bag, and everything fell out all over the counter. That's when you walked in."

"How about if I do it for you? You stay right here, and I'll get what we need."

"Oh, it's *we* now?" she said with a forced smile when she heard the bite in her voice.

"Yes. It's *we* from here on out. So get used to it." I gave her a little wink and went to gather up the supplies from the bathroom counter.

Surprisingly, she turned on the bed to watch my progress but didn't rush over to do it herself. I struggled with deciding to bring up her independent streak now or wait a little. Obviously, she was like an exposed nerve at the moment. Probably only a small fraction of my words would soak through the guard she had raised if I brought up the topic now.

I nudged her over toward the center of the bed with my body as I sat by her side. I spread out the supplies and thought about a fun way to distract her for a bit.

"Okay, young lady." I looked at her mischievously. "If you're a good patient for the doctor today, you can choose a prize from the treasure chest in the waiting room."

Picking up on my game, she quickly sat up. I piled pillows behind her to help her get comfortable.

"I'm not so sure I can sit still, Doctor ... " she said slyly.

"No prize for you, then." I shrugged. "I'd think you would at least try."

"What sort of prizes do you have to choose from?" She giggled.

"You have to wait and see. Only good patients get to peek."

"I'll try my best," she said, but I gave her a skeptical look.

"What?" she whined, and I had to grin.

I was so thankful she wanted to play doctor with me. We used to act out all kinds of role-playing scenarios in our earlier days. I'd definitely been missing it. People let go of all kinds of inhibitions when they had the chance to pretend they were someone else. Right now, my instincts told me she could use more than a little escape, too.

I grabbed a magazine off her nightstand and flipped through the pages. "Your chart says you're here for an injection today?" I looked to her with one brow raised high.

"Yes, that's correct. I come here all the time, though. Why haven't I seen you before?" she asked, getting bolder now as we settled into our roles. "You're very handsome. I'm sure I would've remembered you. What did you say your name is?"

I leaned in very close to her mouth and said, "I'm Doctor Masterson. After today's appointment, I don't think you'll have trouble remembering."

She grinned wide. "Why is that?"

"I plan on making it very memorable." After issuing that promise, I sealed my lips over hers and urged her to part so my exploring tongue could flutter and flick against hers. Already, my cock was at full attention, and the thing throbbed beneath my zipper.

"Now lie back and let me conduct a thorough exam."

Even though she complied, she still said, "But I'm just here for a shot."

"Every good doctor knows you have to assess the patient fully before administering treatment. I don't want to miss a single thing. And more importantly," I said as I began working her black blouse's buttons open, "I want you to leave my office satisfied."

Her eyes were glassy now, and this time from arousal and not because she had been crying.

"Oh . . . " She breathed and let her eyes close.

"*Oh* as in yes, I have permission to touch this incredible body?"

"Yes. Please, Doctor. Do whatever you see fit."

"Good girl," I growled and spread her shirt open wide to expose her pale-blue bra. With a husky groan, I tugged the fabric away from her breast and kissed her silky skin. The taste and smell of this woman's skin woke the animal inside me. It always had. And it wasn't some expensive perfume or bath product—it was her. Cassiopeia Shark. My very one and only.

"I love you, lady," I declared against her perfect nipple. The dusty-pink circle was a shade darker from her arousal, and I continued licking and nipping the perfection. One particular bite was harder than the others, and she moaned into the dimly lit bedroom.

"Jesus, Jake. Feels so good." She wove her fingers through my hair and thrust her breasts into my face.

Hell yes. I nuzzled the skin between her tits and greedily inhaled her. When she tugged my hair harder, I sank my teeth into the underside of her mound.

"Is that what you want, darling? I'll mark this whole body

if you're up for it." I missed the days when her body looked like a roadmap of my pleasure when we were finished. She loved the bite marks and belt welts afterward too and never asked me to stop or go easy on her.

And all the time we were apart, I never found another woman who answered my dominant call the way this woman had. Not even close. There had been a handful of women over the past nine years who tried, but it was always a disappointment for me. They went away completely satisfied, but when those nights were over, I went home empty inside. Empty and alone.

I was thankful for every cosmic force that brought her back to me. Heaven knew how often I begged for the reality.

"Jake. God, yes. Please, please . . . " she issued.

But honestly, I didn't know what she needed. I was giving her everything I knew she liked.

"Tell me, Star. What are you begging for so beautifully?"

"Take it away. Please, take it all away."

I stilled above her. I knew what she was asking for, but we had some complications now that we didn't have before. There were other people in the house currently. The child didn't need more emotional damage than she just took on from being abducted, and the adult had a load of PTSD triggers I didn't want to set off.

"Please," she moaned again while staring up at me.

After kissing her thoroughly—thinking the entire time how badly I wanted to give her what she was asking for—my dick was so hard, it ached.

"Star, listen to me." I waited for her to open her eyes and focus.

She was in a fog of lust and desire, and I wanted nothing

more than to whip up more of the same storm for her. But this deserved a check-in.

Finally, she answered, "What? I thought you said you still ... umm ... wanted to play that way?"

I chuckled at the thought of ever changing. My sexual preferences wiring was as permanent in my psyche as my eye color was physically. I also had a hunch it was genetic in some way, given at least two thirds of my siblings were wired the same way.

And before my mind drifted to any of their bedrooms or, God forbid, our parents', I recentered on Pia.

"My love, there is a child in the house. If I whip you now, she will most certainly hear us. Wren too. I don't think that would be a good idea, given the events of the past forty-eight hours. Do you?"

Sadly, she was already shaking her head before I finished getting the concern out.

"We need to get you a gag." I leaned down and kissed her nose. "Or start sleeping at my place more often."

And that was the end of our conversation. Whether she didn't want to address the second part of my comment or felt my ridiculously hard cock rubbing against her, talking time was over.

We both needed a reprieve from the week's drama, and I was just the guy for the job. Knowing Wren was with Vela and the rest of our crime-stopping posse would soon be home with their wives, I silently vowed to deliver her from the hell we'd been living in the best way I knew how.

For the first time since we reunited, I really went at her hard. Most of the episode was with my large palm covering her mouth so she wouldn't alert the entire neighborhood to what we were doing inside her sedate-looking home. Well, sedate minus the cobalt-blue door. I still got a wide grin every time I walked up the front walk and looked at that expressive entrance.

★ ★ ★

Pia slept hard that night. Both from the restless nights she had beforehand and the incredible sex we had to punctuate the day.

I felt satisfied for the first time in years. Nine to be exact. I promised myself, as I drifted off too, that I would broach the subject of cohabitating when the sun came up. I wanted to be near her all the time. I didn't like the thought of going back to that lonely hotel room in the morning. Even more so, I wanted to be near my woman and our amazing daughter and personally ensure they were safe.

If she even tried to argue that she had her brothers—all three—to keep the women of the house and my heart safe, I'd have reasons at the ready why that wasn't a good long-range plan. Two of the three were going to have new babies in the coming months, and their focus would be on their own families. As it should be. It made sense why they were all so protective of Pia and Vela in the past, but it was no longer necessary.

Daddy was home now, and it was time I claimed what was mine.

CHAPTER FIFTEEN

PIA

Not sure when it happened, but sometime in the night, our daughter had climbed into bed between us and was now fast asleep, pressed against her father's rib cage. I'd been awake for the past hour, and all I'd done since opening my eyes was stare at the two of them.

With the expressionless peace of sleep relaxing their features, they looked even more alike than when they were animated. No wonder I always thought she was so beautiful—she was the spitting image of her father. I felt the damn emotion swelling inside my throat again and dragged in a breath to try to stuff them back where they belonged. I'd cried no less than five times yesterday, and my eyes felt like I'd used a sandpaper face mask as some twisted version of self-care.

My burdened inhalation woke my man, and I winced. Then I lay perfectly still and watched his brain come online. His confused expression turned to the warmest, widest smile when he looked between us and saw our little queen in repose between us. He shot his contented stare to mine and was surprised to find me watching him.

He looked down at Vela and then back to me and pointedly made a questioning face. *How long has she been here?* was my interpretation of the look.

I gently raised my hand, palm facing up, like a one-armed *How should I know?*

We were both grinning, though, so I knew he minded as little as I did that she had crawled in between us while we'd slept.

I would never forgive myself for her abduction. Rationally, I knew it wasn't my fault, but the part of my conscience that held all the parental guilt was currently a churning abyss. I also knew that this wasn't something I could voice to Jacob. He would give me a long, stern lecture about the pointlessness of guilting myself and likely back it up with statistics about child abductions.

Taking her back to school was a big concern, too. I hadn't brought it up yet, but I had serious reservations about it.

I'd enrolled her at the Benning Academy based on their stellar reputation and test scores, first and foremost. The second factor that drew me to the school was their close-knit, family-oriented feel. It would be like one village teaching the children instead of a giant, faceless faction like at a public school.

But how could I trust those people to keep her safe while she was in their care after this happened? I questioned their judgment and ability to identify a threatening situation when it seemed so obvious to everyone in our little posse. The school's attorney had called several times, wanting me to sign a release of liability regarding the mistaken release of a student. They were calling the man an unauthorized family member and whitewashing the entire incident.

They had some nerve. Those three phone calls had come in before we went to get her back, and I wasn't feeling very gracious at the time. I wasn't sure I could consult my own attorney on the matter, either, since the abduction hadn't been reported to the police. I definitely needed to check in with my brother for some guidance on the topic.

Oh my God, my head felt like it was going to burst. So many unanswered questions swirling around inside. Each one just gave way to more.

Vela stirred between us, and we both shifted our eyes to her.

I really hoped she would sleep a bit longer. Not knowing how the past few days were for her was driving me crazy. I still wanted to pepper her with questions about her captor, but I didn't want to cause even more trauma. Again, this is where I would call in a professional who knew the right and wrong way to do this sort of thing. And again, I feared any first reporting authority would be obligated to call the police and CPS. Probably in that order.

For now, for whatever amount of time I could milk out of the morning, I'd lie here with the man I loved and our beautiful child nestled between us. Absentmindedly, I ran my fingers through her chestnut hair, and she exhaled a contented sigh. Snuggling deeper into the covers, I pressed my body against hers. If I didn't maintain physical contact with her, I was convinced she'd disappear again. I never wanted to feel that emptiness or face that fear again.

Jacob placed a hand over mine and held my gaze.

With a slight side tilt, I quietly asked him, "What?"

"I won't ever let you go again, Star. Either of you. I just want you to make peace with that now. I can't bear the thought of walking out that door and going back to that depressing little hotel one more time."

A smile broke free, and I whispered, "Okay."

He smiled too and asked, "That's it? Just okay?"

I was confused. I mean, I was smiling when I said it. Didn't that clearly and concisely sum up my feelings on the matter? "I'm not sure what else you want me to say."

He shrugged, or did the best version of it, while propped up on a bent elbow.

"I thought maybe you'd start with, gee, Jacob, you should move in here with us. We have plenty of space, and we'd feel so much safer with you in the house with us."

My smile grew while watching him squirm a bit. It was rare I got the chance to see the man unsure of himself.

To toy with him just a bit more, I said, "Oh."

"Cass, you're killing me here. Put a guy out of his misery, will you?"

When a giggle bubbled up from my chest, I slapped a hand over my mouth to not wake our girl.

Jake growled low and sexy, "You're lucky she's between us right now, or you'd pay for teasing, Ms. Shark."

"I'm not sleeping," a little voice came from the mound between us.

I shot Jacob wide eyes. *Behave!* I mouthed, knowing she was awake now.

"Good morning, sweetheart," I said and finally gave into the urge to bury my nose in her silky hair.

"Did you sleep well?" her father asked, but Vela said nothing to either one of our comments.

"Are you still sleepy, baby? We'll be quiet if you want to doze off again."

This time when she didn't answer, Jake looked at me and said, "Please answer your mother. It's disrespectful to ignore her when she speaks to you."

I froze in place. Couldn't predict which way this would go. And it certainly wasn't that I allowed my child to speak to me in an uncivilized way—*ever*—but shouldn't we have cut the kid some slack?

Carefully, I watched Jake, and he returned my attention. Did he have the right to mind her? I knew how it felt in my gut, and it wasn't good. But I also knew if he was going to step up and be a father to our child, it couldn't always be sunshine and rainbows.

But that comment came way sooner than I'd expected. I hadn't even agreed to him moving in with us yet.

As he continued watching me for some sort of clue regarding my feelings on his comment, I became more and more agitated. No matter what, I didn't want to have an argument in front of her. I knew that much, at least.

I used to hate when my parents fought. In private, in front of us, in public… It didn't matter. My father's temper was always so volatile, especially when fueled by alcohol. I had to be careful not to project those bone-deep memories onto Jacob.

It seemed like twenty minutes passed while I chewed on that one comment, but really, it had been under a minute. Vela's tiny voice broke the mental lashing I was giving myself.

"Sorry, Mom."

I stroked her hair back from her face and leaned in to kiss her round cheek. "It's okay, baby. None of us feels like ourselves yet. At least I don't."

And when did she start calling me Mom and not Mama?

One simple word would probably go unnoticed by anyone else. But not me. That one title change stabbed into me deeper than her simply not answering. Tears were back instantly, and

Jacob noticed right away.

Again, he gave me a questioning look above where our daughter lay with her eyes closed. I gave a quick shake of my head and knew we'd definitely be talking about this later. I didn't know this man to be anything but invested in my happiness. Therefore, whenever he saw me shed tears, he seemed to go on a personal crusade to right the wrong.

And yes, I loved him for that, too.

Vela stirred again and this time sat up completely. Her hair had been damp when we put her in her own bed last night, so now it looked like a nest of brown silk. That was going to be a battle to comb through, but I pushed the worry aside.

"I'm going to go to my room," she announced and began to crawl out from under the covers and down to the foot of the bed.

"Are you still tired?" I asked while bolting to my feet as well. My movement seemed to surprise her, and she skittered back like she was afraid of me.

Another stab to the heart, and this one already ached so badly, I raised a hand to rub the imagined wound. She didn't answer and left the room dragging a blanket that belonged on her bed.

I looked at Jake, who was sitting up against the headboard watching our exchange.

"She's not herself," I said. "At all. I don't know what to do. Should I follow her?"

"I'm not really sure what the right answer is. I think maybe calling her therapist should be the morning's priority, though."

I was already nodding before he finished his thought. "I agree completely. I just don't want to mess this up, you know?" And a damn tear escaped and burned a path down my cheek before I could swipe it away.

"I'm not sure if this will help, but I remember when it was first discovered what my asshole brother-in-law was doing to Stella. She withdrew, much worse than Vela has been." He held up his hand to stop an interjection. "I know this is significant for Vela. I'm not invalidating that at all. Stella was never as well adjusted as Vela. Never in her entire life, so the difference is noticeable but probably more similar than you think."

"What did your sister do? How did she handle her? I feel like pushing her is the wrong move, but at the same time, allowing her to retreat into herself seems wrong too."

He was in front of me then and pulled me into his strong, safe embrace. As always, the comfort I found there was incredible—and so needed. In my heart, I continued to celebrate that I didn't have to do this alone anymore.

I looked up to find him staring at me and placed my palm on his cheek. "Thank you, Jake. Thank you so much for staying last night and for jumping in with both feet. I'm so grateful I don't have to fight this battle as a one-woman army."

"I told you, Star. Never again. You can always count on me." He leaned down and gave me a soft kiss. I wanted to get lost in the feelings that quickly rose when our bodies came together. It was a much nicer emotional pool than the one I was standing on the edge of with our daughter.

"So what did Cecile do to help your niece?" I reminded him before the kissing turned into more.

God, how I want so much more with this man.

"I know she saw a therapist, maybe even twice a week at first. She still takes her now. Can I ask how long you've been taking Vela?"

After scanning my memory, I said, "It's been close to a

year, I'd say. Last year there was an incident"—I winced at the word but had no other replacement at the ready—"at school, and the writing was on the wall. The girl was going to have major daddy issues if I didn't do something."

"That sounds like an entire conversation on its own."

"Probably. But regardless, that's what prompted me to take her to talk to someone outside the family. She's always had Bas and the guys, as well as Wren, who she talks to about anything and everything. Usually, she will go to one of them before me."

I disengaged from his embrace to find my robe. I needed coffee in a big way.

"I'm glad she's had such a strong support network."

"I am too. At first, I'll admit, it bothered me—or hurt me, more accurately—that she felt more comfortable talking to them instead of me, but I remind myself it's about what's best for her in the long run, not about my fragile self-esteem as a single parent."

"Woman," he issued and pulled me to him using the belt of my bathrobe. "You are anything but fragile. You're a damn warrior, and I'm so proud of what you've accomplished with her and every other part of your life." He kissed my forehead and stayed pressed to my skin for a few beats.

"Thank you. And on most days, I know that. I know I can do anything I set my mind to. I know I'm talented and successful in my chosen career. But when it comes to that child, I'd give it all up to guarantee she will grow up to be a well-adjusted, happy, productive human."

"And when it comes down to it, isn't that what being a parent is all about?" Jacob pointed out wisely.

I nodded a few times. "Absolutely."

"Do you want to hop in the shower?" he asked. "I'll get us some coffee."

"Or vice versa?" I offered. I wanted to call my brother and make sure everyone was okay, and if Jacob took a shower first, I could do that sooner rather than later.

"Up to you, my queen," he said with a wink.

"I'll get the coffee and check on Wren while you shower."

"If you hurry, you can join me . . ." he said, looking hopeful.

Laughing, I pushed at his shoulders. "Go."

In the kitchen, I found my assistant and dear friend puttering about like it was any other morning. She looked up from loading the dishwasher and greeted me.

"Good morning. Did you sleep?"

Was it comical or sad that the question had morphed over the past week from how did you sleep to did you sleep at all? Still, I had a warm smile for one of the brightest parts of all my days.

"Good morning, dear. Yes, I slept like a rock. How about you?"

She nodded with a big smile. "Finally, yes. I must not have moved through the entire night. I woke up with a seriously stiff body, but damn do I feel rested. Finally."

"It's amazing what a good night's sleep can do for us, inside and out," I agreed. "My daughter meandered into my bed at some point in the night, though. We woke up with a snuggly surprise between us." The comment was so normal, I couldn't contain my smile.

"God, please tell me you were dressed." She bugged her eyes out over the rim of her coffee mug.

"What would make you think they came off in the first place?" I tried for incredulous, but based on the look she was shooting me, she wasn't buying it.

"Obviously you haven't looked in the mirror this morning. You want coffee?"

While running my fingers through my bedhead hairstyle, I said, "Yes, and one for Jacob, please. He takes his black."

"Well, that will be easy to remember at least. My brain, while rested, is definitely still foggy from those painkillers."

We continued our conversation while I found the almost empty creamer in the back of the refrigerator.

"How is the pain overall? I know you said you were stiff when you woke up, but I also know that mattress in the guest room isn't the best in the house."

Wren just shrugged. "It's fine. A few more days, and I'll be good as new."

I shook the tall plastic bottle. "Can you add this to the grocery list, please? I don't see a replacement in there. I think the boys must have used this entire bottle over the past few days."

"Well, you all were keeping some long hours. No wonder."

I smiled. "True. True. Thank God for caffeine."

"Where is our queen?" Wren asked. "Still in bed?"

"She went back to her own room a little while ago. I'm surprised she didn't mosey her way out here to see if you were up."

"She definitely wasn't acting like herself last night, but I would be concerned if she had been. I wonder how long it will take for her to bounce back?"

"Well, for one thing, we don't really have many details of what she endured while she was missing. She didn't want to talk about anything on the drive home last night, and I didn't push. I'm calling the therapist as soon as the office opens."

"But Pia, what are you going to tell her? That your child was kidnapped from school by your dead infant brother? And that you didn't see it necessary to contact the authorities?"

I guess I knew how Wren felt about my decisions by those few questions. Judging by the way she was holding me hostage with her stare, they weren't rhetorical either. She wanted answers.

Luckily, she slid Jake's coffee across the counter to me, and I grabbed a cup in each hand.

"You're absolutely right. First conversation I'm having is with my brother. Then the doctor." I gave her a pleading smile, silently begging her to leave the topic there for now. Clearly, I didn't have the answers. "Thank you for making our coffee. I need to take a shower so I can get the day started."

"She's not going to school, is she?" Wren asked.

"Hell no."

My answer came as I was turning toward the bedrooms, but most had been delivered before I saw my child standing in the doorway, dressed for school, backpack in place and shoes expertly tied.

"Why?" she asked plainly.

"Why what, Star?"

"Why did you tell Wren I'm not going to school? It's only Fursday. I looked on the calendar." She already had a bite in her tone, and I tried to quickly figure what the right response was here.

"*Thurs*-day." I repeated the word, putting heavy emphasis on the starting consonant combination.

The dirty look she gave me in response to the correction was familiar, however still unacceptable.

Setting down the coffee cups, I replied, "Excuse me, young lady. Did you just roll your eyes at me?" Now my hands were propped firmly on my hips.

My daughter mirrored my pose and nearly spat, "Yeah, I did. So what?"

"Vela. Shark. Watch the tone."

We were locked in a stare-down for a long moment, and finally, she turned and walked back toward her room. Emotional pain restricted my airway. I waited until I heard her door close before heading toward my own room. I just didn't want another showdown so soon. My hands were trembling when I handed Jake his coffee.

"What's going on?" he asked instantly.

"Your daughter is full of attitude this morning. I'm so worried that anything I say or do will be the wrong thing right now. Make things worse." So much of what I was feeling was rooted in fear. I'd be frustrated on any day with the sassy mouth my darling was currently sporting, but every thought, every feeling, every breath, seemed magnified.

"Do you want me to speak to her?" Jacob asked and took a sip of his coffee.

I was shocked it wasn't cold at that point since I'd talked with Wren much longer than expected.

"Mmm, this hits the spot this morning," he said after a second taste of the brew.

I gave him a tight smile, not able to really concentrate on anything beyond Vela's well-being. And my mounting fear of fucking it up.

If I were honest with myself, I felt some anger now too. Did the man think all of this child rearing was easy? The way he offered to "speak to her," as if we weren't in the middle of a crisis here?

But Jacob knew me too well, and I wasn't used to someone

paying such close attention to my actions and reactions. He set his mug down on the vanity and wrapped me in a perfect hug.

"What's going on? You look like you're moments from a breakdown." He kissed the side of my head while he held me and said, "I mean, I get why you are stressed. It's been a trying few days. But she's home now, Star." He leaned back to get a better look at my face and finished with, "But this seems like more than residual stress."

Calmly and quietly, he waited for me to respond in some way. I knew the moment I tried to speak, my shaky voice would betray me. The tears flooding my eyes wouldn't help me sell the *I'm fine* bit either.

I didn't want to lash out at him but felt dangerously close to doing that. It would be better to kick dirt over the bit about being affronted by his nonchalant offer to help. Three minutes earlier, I was overjoyed that he was partnering with me on the parenthood frontline.

"I'm a mess," I said into his chest. "That about sums it up. If you could just hold me for a little longer, though? It's working wonders for my mounting hysteria."

"My darling, I will hold you every time you let me," he said quietly.

But our moment of tranquility was disrupted when we heard Vela shouting in the hall just beyond my door.

"I'm going anyway!"

Opening the door to my room, we found Wren and Vela in a standoff.

Wren shot her gaze to me, and then Vela swung around to find us there too.

"Hey, hey. What's going on? Why the yelling? And please tell me you weren't yelling at Wren." I reached for my daughter, and she physically knocked my outstretched hands away.

"Don't touch me!"

I froze where I stood. She'd never been physical in anger. With me or anyone else I'd witnessed.

Wren stepped in again. "Vela. No way, girl. You don't swing at your mother. Ever."

"Be quiet! You're not the boss of me." With what looked like utter contempt in her eyes, she turned on Jake and me. "Neither are you!"

And then she went for broke.

"I hate you! Forever, I hate you!"

That gem was spewed right in my face, and I was so shocked, I stumbled to the side so the wall could support me.

"Enough!" Jake said firmly.

Our daughter paused for a beat and truly looked scared. His demeanor was stern but not angry, so she recovered quickly. The moment she assessed there wasn't actual danger here, she went on.

"You can't tell me what to do. I changed my mind! I don't want a daddy. Or a mommy or a Wren. Leave me alone!"

I'd heard all I was willing to when I spoke up. "Vela, I'm only going to say this once, so I advise you to listen. Go to your room this instant. I will come speak with you shortly." My voice was lethally calm, even though my insides were a tumultuous riot.

In through the nose . . . out through the mouth.

It was the only way I'd walk off this battlefield without a critical wound. Focusing on my breathing, I stood with my straight arm extended toward her bedroom and waited for her to follow my instruction.

Wisely, Jacob and Wren let me maintain the commander

role. If our little queen sensed mutiny within the ranks, she'd take advantage of the weakness.

Although, without giving the situation too much scrutiny, this seemed like my precious, confused daughter was acting out of fear and not trying to manipulate us. She always got a little extra crackle in her energy when she knew she had been clever enough to gain the upper hand. Currently, any sort of comparable light was extinguished by an oppressive darkness.

She tried to match my resolve and continued to stare back at me while I waited for her to move. Had to hand it to the girl, she definitely had balls today. What the hell was I in for, though, when she went through puberty?

"Go! Now!"

One last command with the power of two lungsful of air behind it, and she finally moved.

I expected the door slam that came on her heels, so it was completely powerless. Immediately I fell into Jake's arms and cried into his chest. My heart was breaking and racing at the same time. I wasn't even sure if that was possible, but that's what the chaos inside felt like.

"I need to go call my brother," I explained.

Jacob looked unhappy about the statement, and I couldn't figure that out either.

"What?" I barked at him unfairly. I knew in my heart, none of this was his fault.

He didn't hold back explaining himself, though. "I would rather not have to call your brother to get involved every time we have a parenting issue."

"That's not why I want to speak to him, Jacob. If I have to justify every action to you... And I would say this is far beyond a *parenting issue*, wouldn't you?" This co-parenting thing was going to take some getting used to on all fronts. "I've never asked my brother to help me make parenting decisions, and I have no intention of starting now," I added when we just stood motionless.

Wren had retreated to the kitchen right after Jake made that dumb remark.

He dipped his head and asked, "All right. Glad to know that. So why is calling him right now more important than what's going on here? May I ask?"

Jake's words were careful, his demeanor courteous. Why, then, did the whole thing set my teeth on edge? I tried to sound equally calm and polite when I answered this time.

"We talked about it this morning—or wait—maybe that was the conversation I had with Wren." Shit, my brain was so disjointed at the moment. Shaking my head, I apologized. "Sorry. I'm not firing on all cylinders this morning." I tapped my temple with my index finger while offering the explanation.

"You don't have to apologize, Star. There's a lot going on right now."

"But there always is. I think it's the magnitude of what's going on with her..." I gestured with my chin toward our daughter's bedroom. "I need to talk to my brother to find out how much I can and cannot explain to her therapist. That's the objective. Not speaking to my brother for some daily check-in. He just happens to have the puzzle piece that fits between this experience and her therapist. I think that probably should all make sense?"

I ended the explanation with the lilt of a question, but why? Just so my man could give me his stamp of approval? Both that he thought my plan was a solid one, and that he agreed with it in general truly mattered to me, but I was so conflicted that it did.

"You're way better at all of this than you give yourself credit for. You know her so well, and you know the best ways to approach and get through to her. If anyone doesn't see that, they're a fool." Jake said all of that and then slid down the wall beside Vela's door.

Okay, that action confused me. "What are you doing?"

"I'm going to wait here while you make that phone call. I don't want her sneaking out while we aren't paying attention. Can you imagine having her missing again?" He shuddered before finishing his thought. "I can't."

I couldn't help but grin at his overprotectiveness. "Dude, she's eight, not eighteen. I don't think we're in danger of her sneaking out the window of her room just yet."

"I don't think I'd put anything past that clever little mind. She floors me with the level of understanding she has of things going on around her. I know she's often the only child you're around, but I'm telling you, Cass, she's way beyond her years."

Jacob held my stare the entire time he spoke, and I felt the gravity of his concern. If he truly believed she was a flight risk, then there wasn't actual harm in him posting watch outside her door.

After nodding, I bent forward at the waist and gave him a quick kiss. "You know what, Mr. Cole-Masterson?"

Through his smirk, he replied, "What is it, darling?"

"I think I really like having you around."

He grabbed the front of my robe and tugged me back down to his level. "That's good. Because you're not getting rid of me so easily this time. Mark my words."

CHAPTER SIXTEEN

JACOB

When Pia finished her phone call, I finished getting ready for work. I had very few items at her house, so at least there wasn't too much time wasted on deciding which shirt went with which slacks.

"Don't you look all handsome and professional," my beautiful woman said from behind me.

I swung around to find her checking me out with a hungry smile. "Thank you." I closed the small space between us and pulled her into my arms. I could really settle into a life like this. Although these mood swings of hers could totally fuck off. After I stole a kiss . . . or three . . . I asked, "What's your plan for the day? Were you able to get an appointment with the therapist?"

"Yes, I did," she said, tugging at the sleeve of her robe. "She is squeezing us in between two regular clients but was going to try to rearrange some things so no one got screwed out of their appointment time."

"What's wrong, baby? You look uneasy about something." This was the longest I'd seen this woman lounge around in pajamas or a robe—ever.

"I'm kind of dreading this appointment. Not going to lie. I have no idea what our little star is going to come out with on a good day. With her temperament so volatile, I fear one or all of us will be in jail by dinner."

"Maybe try to stay busy until the appointment time?" I offered in suggestion, but it came out more like a question. "Do you sit in the appointment with her?"

"Not usually. Although I'm thinking maybe I should? I don't know. Her therapist is really good at letting me know when I need to be present and when they need privacy. A lot of times, I think our daughter's biggest issues are with me. So she wouldn't feel as free to voice that sort of thing with me in the room, you know?"

"Right. Makes sense. What did your brother advise regarding the amount of detail you should, or could, go into?" I asked while we worked together to make the bed.

"Well, since this person calling himself our brother went so far as to identify himself as such at the school, the cat's pretty much out of the bag. So there's no real need to cover that up and complicate things in Vela's head. I've spent the past eight years preaching to the child about honesty and the value of a person's word. It would be out of character for me to ask her to lie now."

"Yeah, that's a slippery slope for sure. She's smart as a whip, but I'm not sure any eight-year-old has the judgment to discern when it's appropriate to stretch the truth and not."

Pia tossed the last pillow from the bed into place and nodded. "Exactly. I think it would be more confusing than the whole mess already is."

I swallowed hard and reached for her hands, inhaled, and hoped like hell I wasn't blowing a huge hole in every delicate thing we were building between us and asked, "Do you think he did anything . . . " I held her gaze, hoping she would just know what I was getting at.

She just focused on my fidgeting and didn't offer an out.

"I mean, do you think he did anything to her? Like touched her?" Bile repeated in the back of my throat. Churned all the way up from my stomach at the thought of our precious little girl being violated by anyone—ever. The thought made my gut roil while I waited for her input.

"I don't know. And I don't know how to bring up the subject. I hope in my heart that she would've confided in me already if he had, but I've had a real bucket of ice water dumped on me about what I can trust as fact or not with her."

"What do you mean?" I could sense whatever she was talking about held a long round of the blame game too. And the person she was blaming was herself.

She shook her head. "I mean, I would've bet a year's salary that my child knew better than to go anywhere with a stranger. That she possessed enough fear in whatever part of us that is responsible for intuition to be leery of a strange man just bullshitting his way through picking her up at school."

She continued to slowly shake her head from left to right, and when she met my watchful eyes again, hers were filled with tears.

"But I was wrong. So very wrong," she admitted.

It looked like her saying those few sentences tore a part of her heart and possibly her soul away with them.

I held her hands between us and implored, "Please don't do this to yourself. This situation has been difficult to say the very least. Looking for somewhere to lay blame isn't going to make anyone feel better. Especially if you decide you're most deserving of the responsibility. You're an amazing mother, Pia. What I've seen? I'm in complete awe. Please don't discredit all you've done."

It was hard to know if my words were getting through. I knew how thick this woman's head could be when she got an idea in her mind. I also knew that underneath the confident, brave, smart outer version of herself that the world saw on a daily basis was a scared, self-doubting, vulnerable young single mother.

Well, fuck that last one, because I vowed to her and our daughter—and to myself—that they would always have me to lean on now. I would never take off when things were tough, and I would love them to my heart's fullest capacity for the rest of my days.

I kissed her forehead and stayed like that for a moment. Just feeling her warm skin beneath my lips, inhaling that perfectly feminine scent that danced in my memories when I'd lost her.

"I love you," I vowed against her flesh. "I will love you more tomorrow, and more than that the day after. Whatever I can do to help you, Star, it's yours. Say the word, and it's yours."

She pulled back a few inches so we could look into each other's eyes. Pia stared for a few moments, and tears slowly tracked down her flushed cheeks.

"Thank you, Jacob. Thank you for being here right now. Thank you for never giving up on us."

I smiled at her words, and she looked affronted.

"Calm down, Shark. I'm smiling because you say those things like I ever had a choice in the matter. You know we always said we were written in the stars. I still believed that every day we were apart, and it brought us back together. The power of love—our love—is a magical thing."

"My goodness, you're a poet this morning. Thank you for saying such beautiful things."

"I mean them."

"I know you do. I'm starting to remember just how contagious your optimism can be. And I really needed to hear all those things right now. It's not always easy being strong and brave when you're alone."

"You'll never be alone again, Cass. I swear you won't."

In theory and devotion, at least. Because soon after that pep talk, I left for the office. I had a meeting previously scheduled with Sebastian that started in one hour, and if I didn't get on the freeway, I'd never make it. The man hadn't messaged that morning to cancel our appointment, so I'd show up as expected.

There were a million unanswered questions about the previous night swirling in my head as I made my way downtown. Hopefully, the meeting would be just the two of us. But even if the other two attached to his hip were present, I'd get some answers.

Stepping off the elevator with about ten minutes to spare, I went straight for Shark's office. His assistant, Craig, announced my arrival and ushered me inside the expansive suite. Sebastian stood with his back to the room, talking on the phone and surveying his kingdom from the tall windows.

After I set my bag down, I pulled out the latest prints we needed to review and went to set them up on the conference room table. So far, it was just Sebastian and me in the office, and I wished silently that it would stay that way. It always felt like I was facing the firing squad when the three of them stood and stared at me, cracking jokes at my expense.

My typical defense was to pretend I wasn't listening to their banter, but I heard every word. The morning had already been trying enough. I thought if I had to endure the stand-up comedy routine today, someone might leave with a shiner. My skin was pretty thick, having grown up with so many brothers, but these men owed me a certain level of professional respect, if nothing else.

I assumed a lot of the joking was born from their protective tendencies where Pia was concerned. Strangely, I admired that about them, even if it meant that frequently I had to be the sucker with the target painted on his back. For her, I would endure anything. That thought had a wave of calm dousing my growing temper, and I patiently waited for Shark to end his call.

From what I could make out, he was talking to his wife, Abbigail. Now that she was expecting again, Sebastian was even more protective than before. I admired the man for that and could relate to the feeling. The guy had no actual role model growing up but was inherently a good caregiver and attentive-as-hell husband.

While I had the time, I wondered what it would've been like to be by Pia's side while she was pregnant. Would I have worried myself sick over every little ache and pain? Or maybe I would have become more tender and careful and protective against every possible danger?

Those thoughts led me down another path. Did Pia want more children? When I'd asked her about it before, she covered her true feelings with some smart remark like she often did when feeling vulnerable. To me, that meant she did want to add to our small, new family but didn't want to put herself out there and admit it in case I didn't. If she gave a nonanswer, it wouldn't be the wrong answer.

If we got busy trying now, she could go through a pregnancy with the other women of this tight-knit group. Our child would have siblings as close playmates that would turn into lifelong best friends. I'd definitely broach the subject as soon as possible.

"Jacob Cole!" Bas bellowed, and I jumped from my daydream to the present.

"How's it going?" I smiled and offered a hand in greeting.

"Well, you know. Stubborn, pregnant wife. Stubborn, emotional sister. Stubborn—" He chuckled. "Well, just stubborn friends."

"Birds of a feather?" I asked lightheartedly, and he gave me a sideways glare.

I held up both hands in defense. "Come on now. Just joking around." Yeah, this guy didn't have the luxury of nonstop sibling ribbing like I did. His skin was as thin as mine was thick.

"How is my niece today?" he asked, completely changing the subject.

Can't say I wasn't thankful.

"She's definitely not herself. Pia was able to get an appointment with her regular therapist, though, so we're hoping she can give us some insight."

"Insight on what?"

"How to handle her right now. She's very volatile. Angry and scared at the same time. I'd have to think it's all very confusing."

"Poor kid. I'd give anything for her not to have been dragged into the middle of this. It was really shitty of our brother to do that."

"So you think this guy is really your brother?" I asked.

The man folded his thick arms across his chest and leaned against the table. "Checks out so far. Elijah's got an army looking into everything we can find on the guy. Even the most random crap he spewed last night. Lab is testing the blood sample, so we'll know soon enough."

"What's the guy's end goal? Like, what does he want? Did he say? Or did he just keep going on and on with the crazy shit?"

"Money. In the end, it's what they all want. He wants me to pull my vessels out of the lane he uses to dump bodies. Said I'm killing his business, and because he wasn't given the leg up in life that I was, it's the least I can do for him now." He forced a laugh then muttered, "Asshole."

I screwed up my face at that one comment. Based on everything I'd ever heard about the Shark siblings, their childhood was not rosy and grand.

Sebastian answered the question I didn't ask out loud. "I know, he's delusional. I don't know where he's getting the idea from. Everyone knows I had to crawl my way up out of the gutter to get where I am today."

"I suppose if he had it worse, your life may seem rosy?" I speculated, even though I knew Shark wouldn't appreciate my question.

The man shook his head with a huff. "Shit. How much worse could it get? We were left to fend for ourselves. There were weeks . . . I'm not exaggerating . . . weeks where we didn't know how we'd eat. Pia was so small and skinny, I had to hold her in my arms at night when we slept just to keep her warm."

Scanning my memory from the night before, I asked, "Wasn't he rambling about having a mother or something, though? Like the nurse switched babies and he was taken home from the hospital by another woman?"

"Yeah, and I guess that nurse was nuts. Elijah found criminal records. She was selling babies as a side hustle. Looks like she's up north in the women's pen the state runs." Sebastian explained this while fixing a cup of coffee.

When he gestured to the setup, I just held up a hand in response. If I had another cup, I'd be bouncing off the walls.

Shark continued. "And the woman who bought our infant brother was crazy. Probably why she couldn't get a man to knock her up the right way." He chuckled, but I didn't join in. "From what he was saying, she sounded worse than Grant's old lady and Elijah's old man put together. She abused him for entertainment. Let her friends get in on it for kicks, too."

"He told you all that?" My voice cracked with incredulity.

"Yeah. Didn't go into gory, graphic detail—thank fuck—but he said enough to paint a clear picture. If he's lying, he has one hell of a twisted imagination."

I wondered how they had the chance to exchange so much information there on that bike path, but how did I ask that without sounding like I was doubting what he was telling me? Did it really matter how they extracted details from the guy? Probably not. It might even be better for my family if Caleb thought we didn't know his sordid past.

Still, I had so many questions. "Where is that woman now? His adoptive mother? Did he say?"

"Dead," Sebastian answered simply. "Can't be sure, but it sounded like he'd had enough of her bullshit one day and fought back. Killed her."

"How much of this did you tell your sister?"

"None, yet. I wanted to be sure this guy was legit—well, legit as far as backstory—before I told her. I can never predict which way the woman will go with stuff like this. She's a lot like Abbi. Heart so big it gets in the way of sound judgment."

"What do you mean?" If I had to defend my woman here, I wanted to be sure I was understanding him correctly.

"Both women see the best in everyone. Want to give people—even shitbags—the benefit of the doubt. Although, the fact that he fucked with her daughter may have his coffin nailed shut as far as Dub's concerned. But like I said, I can never predict her reactions."

The man had a warm smile for the first time in the entire conversation. I wasn't sure if it was mentioning his wife or his sister that elicited that reaction, but Sebastian Shark definitely had a soft spot for both.

I nodded while he explained. I agreed with the points he made, especially how fucked up it was that their supposed brother chose to terrorize our child as a way to get to Bas. It probably doomed him forever in Pia's eyes. It certainly would be a cold day in hell before I forgave the guy.

"I had to explain the abduction to my parents," I tossed out. There was no sense sugarcoating anything at this point. We were all dealing with a big heap of trouble with this guy making demands, and they had every right to know what was going on. I wouldn't apologize for it. "They'll likely want to press charges or settle the score with the guy in one way or another. My father doesn't look kindly on criminals."

Sebastian was thoughtful for a few moments and didn't give away what he was contemplating by his expression. Not even a little. So I waited for him to loop me in.

"Look, I'm not defending the guy, and I'm trying to think of another way to word what I want to say so it doesn't come across that way. But I got nothing. Shit, I'm so fucking tired." Shark dragged a heavy hand down his face. "The baby has kept us up night after night, and then there's Abbigail's nausea when we do finally fall asleep. Anyway . . . "

He made a sour face, and I chuckled.

"What's funny?"

"Not funny..." Then I thought about it again. "Well, I guess that's not true. It's kind of funny hearing you complain about such pedestrian things, you know? You sort of have this big, bad, powerful guy persona you put out into the world. Hearing that you're just as affected by the regular trappings of life?" I shrugged and just shut up there. Probably wasn't making much sense to him anyway.

"I put my pants on one leg at a time, just like you," Bas said and then laughed. "And with you, I can't even say they're just nicer pants, because coming from the family you do, I doubt that it's true."

All I could do was shrug. When I was younger, I felt tremendous guilt about my family's wealth. Not anymore. Once I was out on my own and earning a legitimate living, it really drove home how hard my parents worked. They were excellent role models in that regard.

"But what were you going to say...before mentioning your family?"

"I guess I can't piece together why your folks would feel the need—or the right, more so—to prosecute the guy. I'm not saying the asshole doesn't deserve it, but why would they assume that responsibility? He did nothing to them."

"That's my father's way of handling things. He's a take-charge kind of guy and was always the one everyone went to when something had to be fixed. Add in too many years making the corporate world his priority..." I shrugged and wondered if I was making sense. "When things happen in his personal life, he thinks they are handled the same way."

Then I thought of a perfect way to explain what I was saying and barked out a laugh much too loud for the setting.

"I'm surprised he doesn't look at weddings as mergers and childbirths like asset accumulation."

"Abbi will make sure I don't treat our kids that way. Now that she's decided to sell her business, she's all about the family unit being top priority."

"Oh, I didn't realize she was selling her catering business. That's a shame. Pia said they've really had some intense growth over the past few years. It must've been a hard decision to come to—selling when they are doing so well." And suddenly it felt so good to be talking about something other than abductions and crazy not-dead brothers.

"Well, she sold her half of the business to her partner, Rio. Grant's wife?" he explained and asked the last part to be sure I was keeping up with the who's who.

"Interesting," I said while thinking of the bits and pieces I knew about that woman.

"Interesting how?"

"I thought I heard Grant talking about also trying to start a family. Sure, selling gives your wife a break, but won't that double down on Grant's? And Elijah's wife works there as well, right?"

Sebastian nodded. "Hannah. Yes, she does, and yes, she's also pregnant at the moment. In about four or five months, the infrastructure of that company will be a hot mess."

Jokingly, I said, "They could always add on a nursery and just bring the kids to work."

"Hell no," he said sternly. "And don't you dare say that out loud when my woman is nearby. The buyout hasn't been inked yet, and I don't want her getting any wild ideas."

He wasn't even trying to sell his reaction as a joke.

"What do you say we get down to business here?" I finally

offered before we ended up arguing about a topic it appeared we didn't agree on.

I loved that Pia had her own successful career in addition to being an outstanding mother. Knowing her personality and drive, I couldn't imagine she would be content staying home all day, every day.

I added that topic to the ever-growing mental list of things we needed to talk about, because maybe I had it all wrong. Maybe she worked because she had to in order to support herself and our daughter. Maybe she would like to stay home too.

Concentrating on the prints in front of us, we discussed the tower phase of the Edge and worked on projections for opening a sales office and residential models. Shark planned to option the units for lease or purchase, and the sooner he could start getting traffic through the space, the better for revenue stream.

"These would be really good questions for Pia," I said at one point. Many of the things we were discussing involved her design team and trying to estimate timelines for things neither one of us specialized in. We would end up having to refigure our entire schedule depending on her expert forecasts.

"I'll call her," Bas said while striding toward his desk to make the phone call. "Then we can wrap this up."

"No. I wouldn't call her now," I said to stop him.

The death glare the man had on his face when he turned back to face me would've made another man cower. Instead, a grin broke out on my lips and kept spreading the longer he stood there pouting.

I'd mentally compared him to a child so many times since knowing him. His current state was just priceless supporting evidence to my opinion. He was used to getting his way on all things. There was some perverse satisfaction in being the one to stop him in his tracks.

Finally, when he twitched one too many times, I explained, "I told you she's taking Vela to the therapist. I just think it's bad timing. Even if she's still at the house, I'm sure they will be leaving soon. Also, I think she would want to keep her focus on Vela and everything she's dealing with. That makes sense, right?"

Maybe I shouldn't speak for her, especially with regard to a professional matter. But instead of letting insecure thoughts like that whittle away at my resolve, I put trust in my gut and my heart. I knew her. Knew her damn well, as a matter of fact. She would say the same thing to her brother if she were here.

Additionally, she had an entire staff who worked for her. If we really needed something settled here and now, I was sure one of them could step in and advise us.

I entertained myself by counting the number of times I saw his jaw pulse while he decided how to respond. There was no way I'd roll over, though. Our daughter had to be the center of our focus until we were sure she wasn't permanently fucked up from the abduction.

The same abduction that was executed as a means to flush out her uncle.

Finally, he dipped his chin toward his chest and sighed. "I'm sure you're right."

Saying those few words probably took a few years off his life, but he survived the admission. He caved with less than ten seconds of tolerance left from me. I'd been coaching myself since this whole mess started not to stomp around pointing fingers. But if I indulged the memories clamoring around my mind for even a moment longer, I'd be ready to flatten the guy.

"We had a pretty rough morning at the house before I came here," I offered, finally giving the man a little insight as to what this was doing to his sister and her family.

"Sorry to hear that. I know my sister can be a handful," he replied.

I shook my head. "Nah, it's not Pia. That woman is a saint. And a damn warrior. It's Vela. She's really messed up from the abduction, and we're hoping like hell the therapist can give us some insight on how to handle her and not do more damage." Okay, so that was more than I intended on sharing, but once I started talking, it all just poured out.

"Damage? Aren't you being a bit dramatic? She's a kid, for Christ's sake. Kids are resilient and all that." He waved his hand through the air like he was swatting away a pesty fly.

If only it were that easy.

"How many kids do you know who have been kidnapped? As retaliation against someone they love? It's not a common thing, man. She's angry and scared and lashing out at everyone who tries to show her love or compassion."

"I'm sure she'll be just fine in a few days. Pia has a really good shrink she takes her to. I checked the lady out when she first started seeing her."

My face was twisted with disappointment. I could feel it, and based on the way Shark was staring at me, he could see it. What would it hurt the guy to admit this was all his fault? Just once . . . take ownership for the messes he'd caused in so many of the lives around him.

"Well, I think we're probably done here for the day?" I figured getting out of the same physical space was my best bet. "I'll schedule our next meeting with Craig, and I'll talk about the timing of some of these action items with Pia tonight."

"So, what? Are you just moving in with them? Sounds like you're staying there an awful lot."

And that was it. The verbal straw that broke the camel's back. I was done playing nice with the man.

"That's not really your business, is it?" I fired back.

"Everything involving my sister is my business," he said smugly.

"Not anymore," I said with a shrug and a smirk, and I could see how much the almighty Sebastian Shark didn't care for my answer.

Well… too fucking bad.

I left without another word and without a friendly farewell. On the other side of his heavy door, I finally exhaled and caught the attention of his assistant. Yeah—I wasn't in the mood for this guy either, so I strode straight to the elevator. Luck was finally on my side, and the thing was on the top floor when I pressed the call button.

Once inside the lift, I really took a few steadying breaths and let my briefcase flop to the floor. It made so much sense why Pia hid who her family was in college. If this guy was this much of a controlling asshole *about* her, I could imagine how he acted *to* her.

Like I told him, those days were done.

CHAPTER SEVENTEEN

PIA

Two weeks later, we were doing much better. Well, I thought we were. In reality, the moody child's outbursts were becoming the new normal, so it seemed like things were better when they stopped progressively getting worse.

Jacob had moved his small amount of belongings in over the past weekend, and we stood side by side at the bathroom mirror and dressed for work. I sneaked glances at him every chance I could, and on the last peek, I was busted.

He wrapped his arms around my waist and pulled me into his body. He smelled so good, I buried my face in his chest and thanked the stars that I hadn't put on makeup yet or I would've had to pass on the indulgence.

"I'd be a very happy girl to spend my day like this," I mumbled into his shirt.

"Although we'd both have a lot of disappointed clients to answer to, I'd love nothing more," Jacob said and pressed his growing dick into me.

"Does this thing ever settle down fully?" I teased and rubbed the front of his slacks with my palm.

"Not with you around, Ms. Shark, and oh, shit...yes... feels so good..." He totally dropped the rest of his thought and enjoyed my busy work.

"As much as I'd love to spend my day doing this too, we're going to be late if we don't stop." When he dropped his grip from my hips, I stepped away from him and hurried into my closet.

He groaned when I scurried away, and his deep, lusty sound vibrated through to my core.

We were like damn teenagers again, and no matter how many times he took me, I wanted more. Maybe we were making up for lost time?

Yeah, I'll go with that.

Maybe we were using our reunion sex as a balm on our battered hearts at the end of every day that felt like our daughter was slipping through our fingers.

"What does your day look like?" Jacob called to me while I was still in my closet. "Can we have lunch together?"

"Mmm, I don't think so. I have a lunch appointment already scheduled. I'm sorry, baby." I emerged from my walk-in to find him pouting in the middle of the bedroom. I couldn't hold back my giggle at his dramatic disappointment. I also hoped to not have to share that I was meeting with my brother today.

"The days drag by when I don't see you in one capacity or another. Although I can't say I'm disappointed I don't have a meeting with your brother today."

"When are we all getting together again? Later in the week, I think?" I asked, not having my schedule committed to memory like he usually did.

"Yep. Thursday, I believe. And don't forget we're having dinner at my parents' tomorrow night."

I was the one to groan that time, and there was nothing sexy about the sound. I wasn't looking forward to the date. In fact, I was dreading it. I was convinced the elder Mastersons disliked me before they even met me. No matter what Jacob said to convince me otherwise, my opinion wouldn't budge.

"I know you're not happy about the dinner, Star, but I appreciate you doing it for me. They really want to get to know you and Vela, and I think it shows a lot of effort on their part. At least from the way I've seen them behave in the past with any of my siblings' significant others."

With a big lump of dread in my chest, I asked, "See what I'm stressing about? When you say things like that. I know that was meant to reassure me, but it has the opposite effect."

"It'll be fine. You'll see. They're going to love you almost as much as I do." He smiled and kissed the tip of my nose. "Let's see if our queen is ready to go."

And this was the part of the morning we'd come to dread. We never knew which version of our daughter we'd encounter on the other side of our bedroom door. Some days we were closer to the old temperament than others, but mostly, we were still miles away.

Though she begged nearly every morning, I still hadn't taken her back to school. I offered to invite friends over for playdates on the advice of her therapist, but she refused. She said she was missing out on classroom instruction, and Jacob and I both stared at her like she was from Mars. What child was more concerned about learning than socializing?

Part of me suspected it was her attempt at manipulating the situation, to make me feel more guilty than I already did that she was missing school. But her doctor reassured me that taking her back to that building alone had the potential to trigger memories she didn't even know were hiding beneath the surface.

One of the many things on my to-do list for the day was to call Benning Academy and set up a site visit when the student body wasn't present. If she melted down, it would be private and contained and as controlled of a situation as we could manage.

We'd already had several public meltdowns, and each one was more intense than the one before. It was almost like the strain on her little mind was compounding instead of dissipating, and the fear of what was to come kept me awake at night.

Jacob held on to monumental resentment toward my brother for getting our daughter in this situation in the first place. Privately, Vela's therapist explained to me that it was human nature to find a reason for bad things happening, and Sebastian was the obvious target in this mess. Bad things made more sense when the brain had a place to assign blame.

Maybe because I'd been so close to Bas our whole lives, I was used to people targeting him for one reason or another. I didn't see what good would come of blaming him for what happened to our daughter, though deep down, I agreed with my boyfriend.

But I stuffed those thoughts away and focused on the present. All I wanted now was to have my vivacious, beautiful, smart, witty child back. I prayed that version of her wasn't gone forever.

"Hey, what's up?" Jake asked, noticing my mood shift.

"Just thinking." I tried to fake a smile but came up shy.

"Still about the dinner with my parents? Darling, if it's going to give you that much stress, I can cancel. I mean, we're going to have to bite the bullet eventually, but maybe it's too soon for you after everything..."

He trailed off there because neither of us could bring ourselves to say certain keywords out loud regarding our child's abduction. One comforting discovery that had come from her sessions thus far was we didn't think she'd been molested or physically abused in any way while in my estranged brother's care.

And yes, the man was definitely of the same genetic makeup as Bas and me. The lab reports came in right away after that miserable night and proved the man was who he claimed to be. The question now was what did we do with that information?

Caleb basically disappeared after the night in Long Beach. Bas suspected we hadn't heard the last of him, though, and I agreed to a ramped-up security presence around my entire family.

When I'd asked Sebastian if he planned on pulling his freighters from that shipping lane, he'd scoffed like I'd suggested Santa Claus serve on his board of directors. Telling Jacob that information had launched an argument of monumental proportions, and I still didn't really know what we were fighting about.

I'd agreed with him that Bas was being a careless ass and that it was easier for him to be so cavalier about the whole topic because it hadn't been his child who had been taken to prove a point. It had been ours. We'd ended that night in tears for me and a whole lot of grumbling and stomping around for Jake.

And that led us right back to the ongoing debate about Vela returning to school. If Sebastian didn't meet the guy somewhere on common ground, who was to say Caleb wouldn't target her again?

There had been no actual consequence for her school for

letting my child go with a madman, so did they really learn their lesson? No policy change information had been emailed since the incident, so my guess was they weren't taking it seriously. Or at least as seriously as we thought they should.

Then there was my sweet, capable, kind, and devoted assistant. Since Jacob moved in with us, I noticed Wren retreating. It broke my heart to see her shift herself to the second row, and I'd tried broaching the subject with her. Of course, she said she was doing no such thing and that we couldn't get rid of her that easily, but even my man noticed she hadn't been in the main house as often as she used to be.

The accident did a number on her confidence to drive, especially with Vela in the car. When I'd offered to make her an appointment with my therapist, she laughed. Actually laughed out loud. She followed the reaction up with some comment about scaring her into another profession and promptly left the room.

I knew she wasn't a fan of psychology professionals, but if she didn't face her fear of being behind the wheel with my child in the car, it would negate a lot of her usefulness in my daily life. Our friendship would always be something I cherished, but I needed her help with Vela too.

Outside my bedroom door, the morning showdown began. I swung the thing open swiftly and caught my daughter just before she hurled another inappropriate insult at her caregiver.

Wren looked like she'd been up all night—again—and her patience was paper thin. There were going to be some changes starting this moment.

"Vela. Shark," I said and mentally braced myself for her eye roll. "If you take that tone with Wren one more time, I'm going to wash your mouth out with soap. Do. Not. Test. Me. Child."

She stared back at me with wide, defiant eyes.

"Why do we start every morning this way? Can you explain to me why you think it's okay to speak to Wren the way you've been?" I stood with my hands planted on my hips and waited.

Every morning, she shocked me a little more with the venomous things that came out of her eight-year-old mouth.

But something snapped this morning. Instead of the vile, cruel things she'd been spitting at us, she just looked at me. Wordless and lost. I watched her big blue eyes—that were so much like my own—fill with unshed tears.

"I'm so angry," she croaked. Tears spilled onto her cheeks, and she whimpered. "I'm angry and scared, and no one can fix it." I wanted to rush to her and wrap her in my arms, but I sensed it wasn't the time yet. "Why did my uncle scare me like that, when uncles are supposed to be good and love you? What did I do wrong?"

And that was my breaking point.

I dropped to my knees in front of her so we were at the same eye level. "You did nothing wrong. Do you hear me? And it's okay to be angry. You *should* be angry that he did that. I'm angry. Your father's angry."

She looked past me to where Jacob hovered in the doorway.

"Your uncles who adore you and worked day and night to help me find you are angry too," I added.

She crashed into me with her noticeably thinner frame, and I wrapped my arms around her to support her weight.

"I don't want to feel like this anymore. It hurts inside, and it won't go away," my child sobbed into my shoulder.

Instinctively, I rocked her in my arms, trying to calm her with movement like I did when she was a fussy infant.

"Baby, I know. But it will get better." I stroked her matted hair and repeated the promise. "It will get better."

"When?" she demanded with a muffled sob. "When will I stop hurting inside?" She thumped her little fist on her chest. "And when will I forget his ugly face?" She wailed, and it was nearly unbearable, but I knew she had to get all this out.

This breakdown was two weeks in the making, and now that it was upon us, all I could do was rock her in my arms and make promises I had no idea how to keep.

Jacob dropped to the floor beside us, and I held my arm out to Wren too. In an instant she was on Vela's other side, and we all swayed back and forth on the hallway floor.

I met Jacob's stare over our daughter's head, and he looked so distraught, I wanted to hold him too. Watching our daughter go through this emotional storm was breaking him to pieces. The only reason I was holding my shit together was for the sake of my child. I hoped against all hope that when her inner turmoil was all out in the open, we could finally work on repairing the damage.

I had no concept of time while we sat there sharing tears and hugs and random statements about our feelings. This whole experience was so unfair to thrust upon a child so young. Just when she would calm down, she would get hysterical all over again. By the time she was finally quiet, she was completely spent.

Wren and Jake had pulled away from our huddle and looked at Vela from different angles. They both agreed she had exhausted herself into sleep, but I didn't want to disturb her.

I'd sit here all day with her in my arms if it meant we would never have to revisit this nightmare again.

I had been so fearful that Vela blamed me, or worse, Jacob, for what happened. Through all her hysterical ramblings, though, she didn't say that once. Maybe I shouldn't have gotten the amount of relief from that singular fact that I did, but the possibility had scared me more than I admitted to anyone.

Thank God she didn't hold us responsible for her abduction, because I didn't think we would ever be able to shake that blame if she laid it at our feet. It would follow us around and rear its ugly head in every argument and every battle of wills.

And with my child's strong, Shark-style personality, I knew there would be many more of those throughout her adolescence. But if we got through this experience, an argument about a skirt too short or makeup too dark would seem like child's play.

Very softly, Jacob asked, "Do you want to lie down with her? I'll lift her."

I gave a quick nod, and he bent low to take her sleeping form from my arms. Every bone in my body ached when I stood and followed them into our room. I was exhausted too and barely cared that I had appointments at the office I would miss. But if I knew her as well as I thought I did, Wren would call my assistant at my office and let her know I wasn't coming in.

Quietly, I asked Jake to see if she'd handled that for me. He was back in our room and climbing in bed on the other side of our child within minutes.

"She was already on the phone when I went into the kitchen. I feel bad for her, though, because I don't think she should be out there alone. You know? This has been very hard on her too."

"Would you mind if she joined us?" I asked, not knowing if it was asking too much of him to share this time with our dear Wren. "She's like family to Vela and me. I promise it won't be weird." I winced. I didn't even know if he was thinking along those lines.

"I'll go get her. Be right back." He kissed me softly and was off to get the young woman.

They returned together, and she looked like a fish out of water, so I reassured her. "Will you lie down with us, please? I need to feel all my baby chicks in the nest for a while."

That was all Wren needed to hear to coax out a small smile while she toed off her shoes beside the bed.

"Well scoot over," she whispered, but I shook my head.

"No, you go here." I pointed between Vela and me, and Wren climbed under the covers.

I scooted in behind her, and Jake joined us on the other side. Thank God I'd bought a giant bed all those years ago.

We ended up napping together for hours, and I finally felt like I got some restorative sleep. My nights had been fitful and frustrating, and I was officially counting caffeine as one of the main food groups now.

It was just before noon when Jake helped me remake the bed while we discussed what the rest of the day would look like.

"I don't regret spending that time with my girls this morning. Not one bit. But I think I'm going to head into the office and attempt to salvage at least two of the appointments I canceled."

Automatically, I apologized. "I'm sorry."

"Didn't you just hear what I said?" He stopped what he

was doing and held my gaze from across the bed.

"Yes, of course I did."

And now I was in for a lecture. I resisted rolling my eyes, though, since I'd been on the receiving end of the gesture so often with my child. It could be infuriating.

"Then why are you apologizing?" he persisted.

"Habit?" I chuckled a little at my own absurdity, and simultaneously new thoughts launched from that one.

How many times did I do that in a day? Apologize for something I had nothing to do with or that wasn't really wrong in the first place. Of all the things to offer as small talk, how did an apology become my go-to? While most people filled conversational gaps with talk about the weather or how the local sports teams were doing, I apologized for things I didn't do.

Thankfully, my guy changed the subject. "What about you? Does Vela have therapy this afternoon?"

"No, it's an off day. Honestly, I'm glad. I don't think either one of us can handle much more today. I was thinking about hitting the mall, though."

"Will she be okay with that?" he asked while stuffing things into his bag. "I mean the crowds and just being in public in general."

"Well, I want to see her get back on the horse, you know? Her doctor said it may take some coaxing at first, but I really don't want to see her become a recluse." It wasn't like I hadn't thought of all the possible triggers we'd encounter.

"That all makes sense. But I wonder if the mall is too crowded a place to start your effort?"

Why was he second-guessing my decisions on this? I was trying not to let it piss me off, but every time something like this came up, that was the exact reaction I had. Reminding myself to stay calm, I also remembered to cut myself some slack. I'd spent almost nine years doing this myself. Sharing the parenting duties still wasn't a natural fit for me.

After watching me stew, Jacob said, "Don't get mad now because I made a suggestion. You know I will always yield to you where she's concerned. I just thought to mention it, that's all. It wasn't an indictment of your parenting abilities. Sometimes two heads are better than one."

Damn the guy for knowing me so well. At times like this, at least. Other times it was one of the things I celebrated most about reconnecting with him. Our relationship worked so easily because we knew each other so well.

"I'll suggest it to her and see how she reacts. If she seems hesitant, we'll go somewhere else. Maybe the bookstore. I know there is a new book out in her favorite series, so that might entice her enough to get past whatever discomfort she's dealing with."

"There you go! Problem solved. See? This is why you're the mama. Mamas know best, right?" He offered the comment with a genuine smile, but I couldn't match one of my own to it.

I used to think that. I had a lot more confidence in my parenting prowess before my child was stolen right out from under my nose.

I walked with Jacob toward the front door, prattling on as we went. "I was thinking about something else earlier. How unfair is it that something that lasted for no more than three days is taking so long to get over?"

In some respects, I felt like life would never return to normal. We'd always be looking over our shoulders, always acting extra vigilant where her safety was concerned. From the very little I knew about Hannah's experience, the woman said it had changed her entire life. And her abduction was just an attempt!

Then I switched topics again. "Why wasn't there any way to prosecute this guy? Are we doing all we should be doing to ensure this never happens again? What if he goes after one of the other children?" I was ramping up to hysterical, and my man knew it.

Jake answered this one right away. "Your brother seems to think Caleb is done terrorizing him and everyone close to him. What he's basing that on, I'm not sure. But maybe he'd feel more comfortable talking to you about it. Especially if he thought you were still feeling unsafe."

"When we see him on Thursday, I'll bring it up. Maybe Caleb said something in particular. At this point, I'll take any reassurance regarding her safety I can get. Well, everyone's safety is important to me, but hers is what's keeping me up at night. Well, partly, at least."

The second he reached for my hands, I knew I shouldn't have mentioned my sleeping habits. It was becoming a dead horse he beat every morning when I looked like a zombie and considered mainlining coffee straight from the pot.

But instead of the lecture I expected, he patiently explained, "I know you're overtired, so you're not putting pieces together you normally would. We couldn't prosecute the man because then we'd have to involve the authorities. At the time of the incident, we all agreed that wouldn't be in our best interest."

"You're right, you're right," I easily agreed. For one thing, it was the truth. Secondly, it steered him away from nagging me about my lack of sleep.

Jacob leaned in for a kiss goodbye, and I stood in the open

doorway and watched him leave until I couldn't see his car anymore.

Time to go take on the day. Or what was left of it, anyway.

CHAPTER EIGHTEEN

PIA

Sebastian sat behind his computer monitors like he did every other day. I'd been losing patience waiting for him to wrap up the phone call he was on but had to remind myself that the rest of the world wasn't in the crisis I was. Business went on as usual for Shark Enterprises.

Finally, I heard his goodbye and stood to greet my brother. He strode around his desk and took me in a solid hug then immediately held me at arm's length.

"Dub. You have to take better care of yourself or you're going to end up in the hospital. You know better ... "

I sagged in his hold and implored, "Bas, please. Not today, okay?"

"You know you won't be any good to anyone if you crash."

He was serious and sincere, but I ducked out from under his hold. My shoulders ached where he had had me in his strong grip, and I rubbed at the one side. The tempo of the throbbing pain matched the drumbeat in my temples as I slowly exhaled.

"Why don't we sit?" he asked with a brow raised nearly to his hairline.

He kept a careful watch on me as we moved toward the leather sofa, as if I might faint or completely fall to pieces. Second only to Jacob, my brother knew me better than anyone did.

I sagged gracelessly onto the furniture while my brother continued to eye me.

"Stop staring at me," I said and leaned my head back and enjoyed the coolness of the leather. With my eyes closed, I hoped for a reprieve from the pain in my head. I tracked my brother's movements by sound as he joined me in the seating group.

"You okay?" he carefully asked.

"Headache. Bad."

"I can get you some—"

I cut him off there with a raised hand because I'd just popped a couple pain relievers while in the elevator on my way up to his penthouse suite. I dropped my hand to the sofa beside my thigh with a thud.

We sat in silence for a few minutes until the tension grew so thick, even the mighty Shark couldn't take it.

"Pia, tell me what's going on. You're starting to worry me."

I opened just one eye and still managed to glare at him. I was just too exhausted to make both eyes work, especially in tandem. "What do you think's going on? I'm living in legitimate hell with my daughter at the moment. I'm terrified I'm going to fuck her up worse if I make the wrong decision when handling her."

Christ, how could he be so dense? Did he really think everything would just go back to normal because she was back home?

"Spoke to Elijah today. He said he has a team in place at Benning, so anytime you want to send her back, he has the site covered," my brother offered optimistically.

"Thank you. I appreciate the extra eyes on her. Not really sure when she'll be ready to return, though. Or if it will be to that establishment."

"Sure, no worries. Whenever you decide. Whatever you need, Dub. You know that. How is she doing, anyway?" he asked with a much brighter tone. "It's been what? Two weeks? Probably pretty much forgotten by now I would think."

Slowly, I came to a normal sitting position and gaped at him for a long moment. I was at a complete loss as to how to respond to his last comment because everything that sprang to mind was wildly disrespectful.

"Why aren't you saying anything?" he asked and shifted restlessly in his seat.

I bolted to my feet, anger rocketing adrenaline through my body. "Are you serious right now? I'll warn you now, I'm not in a joking mood, so just be fucking serious right now, Sebastian!"

"Why are you yelling? Shit, if you and junior had a fight, don't take it out on me. Or is this hormonal? I'm getting enough of that at home these days to last me a lifetime. I don't need it from you too." He stood up to pace.

After staring in his direction for a bit, I finally said, "You know, I've heard strangers accuse you of being out of touch with the real world ... with the stuff going on right under your nose ... and I've always defended you. But honestly, Bas, that was the dumbest thing that may have ever come out of your self-centered mouth."

Oh, I knew I was playing with fire with my words, but I was so exhausted and so tired of tiptoeing around everyone. If people didn't want to see the harshness of the reality I was dealing with, they could find somewhere else to look.

My sibling returned my stare for much longer than I would've expected after hurling that insult his way. When he finally did speak, it was in the calmest, most controlled tone.

From his mien alone, I knew he was thoroughly pissed.

Smugly, he said, "Did you want to elaborate on that rude remark, or just toss it out and let me make of it whatever I will?"

"I don't have the energy to argue with you today," I sighed.

"Good. I'm not looking for a fight either. But if you're going to insult me, I'd at least like to know why. Seems fair, right?"

Fine. I'd spell it out for the guy. He probably wouldn't like what he was about to hear, though.

"Can you really be so naïve to think that your niece is just fine? I don't think she'll ever be fine again at the rate we're going. How could you say something so thoughtless? I mean, look at me, Bas! I haven't slept since the day she went missing. I feel and look like a zombie!" I took a deep breath before adding, "And stop calling Jacob *junior*! It's condescending and disrespectful. But I suppose that's what you've been aiming for when you use that nickname. Best to keep everyone in their rightful places, am I right?"

"What the hell has gotten into you?" he asked with his face twisted with confusion. "Where is all this coming from?"

"Where do you think?" I asked while still shouting. And damn it, it felt so good to open up on someone. This just happened to be the person who needed to hear the truth the most.

"Listen up, sister of mine. If you scheduled this appointment with me just to use me as a punching bag, I think I'm going to take a pass. Unless you explain to me what's going on, maybe you should head home. Or better yet, I'll have Joel take you. I don't think you should get behind the wheel." He studied me closely like I was an angry cornered bear, and finally, he was getting the gist of the mood here.

"See? That's your problem. Or one of them," I continued

to lecture the clueless guy. "You think you know what's best for everyone, but in reality, it's only to box them into what you can handle. Or control, more like."

Yeah, this feels really good to get this crap out into the open. He approached me in careful increments. "Seriously, Pia. Maybe your sugar is out of whack. Do you have your testing kit with you? You're not making a lot of sense right now."

If possible, I grew angrier with every dumb comment my brother made. In his mind, I couldn't possibly have legitimate gripes or messy emotions. There had to be a logical explanation for it, and blaming my Type 1 always came in handy.

"No. If you'd stop and actually listen to what I'm saying, I'm making perfect sense. You have no idea what that pointless abduction has done to my child and my household. Nor have you cared enough to find out. You just want to hear someone say things are all better now so you can go on with your day like nothing ever happened. Keep your hands nice and clean from the messy stuff and walk away the hero, right?"

"Okay, that's not true. Not at all. I've asked how Vela's doing repeatedly. If it wasn't to you, I asked your new housemate."

"He's her father, Bas! You can say his name. Why do you insist on getting in the little digs every chance you can? Yes, I've asked him to live with us. Yes, it may seem soon to people outside our relationship. I love him. I've never stopped loving him. Is it so fucking wrong for me to want to have a family and be happy? Or is that just something you get to have until you deem me ready? Or maybe in your judgmental mind, I'll never be worthy?"

My brother just shook his head, seeming like everything I accused him of surprised him. I knew he was clueless, but really, was he *that* clueless?

"Dub, honest to God, you're acting crazy right now. Maybe I should call Jake to come pick you up?"

I cackled loudly at that one. And yep! Sounded exactly like the crazy person he just compared me to. "Oh, take it from me, brother, he's the last person you'd want to drag into the middle of this conversation."

"What the hell is that supposed to mean?" His question was backed with a fair amount of anger now.

"He's livid with you, too, but doing a much better job at holding it all in. How can you not see how many people's lives have been fucked to hell because of you? Yet you just saunter around up here in your fancy penthouse office"—I did a little twirl around where I stood, making sparkly fingers at my surroundings—"insisting people are being dramatic when they're emotional about picking up the pieces of the fucking mess you've made."

"Okay, okay. I hear what you're saying. I mean, how could I not? You're screaming like a madwoman. Things are harder than I thought they would be by this point for Vela. Maybe I should've inquired more, but Dub, give me some credit where credit is due. I've been asking. And while you're admitting you haven't exactly been as perfect as you think you are about everything, admit that when I asked about Vela, you've been whitewashing the responses and not telling the truth. So how the fuck was I supposed to know?"

"Don't you fucking yell at me right now. I'm likely to kick you where it counts."

Sebastian scoffed and turned away from our conversation. "This is ridiculous. You're being hysterical over literally nothing."

"Nothing?" My mouth hung open in disbelief. It took

half a minute to find words in the anger fog clouding my brain. "You think my child's life is nothing? Her mental health? Her general well-being?" I shook my head, sickened by his shitty attitude.

"That's not what I meant, and you know it."

"Isn't it? And what about Grant?"

"What about him?" He screwed his face up with indignation.

Did I really need to spell this out for him? His head was farther up his ass than any of us knew.

"Grant? Your best friend? The one who was also abducted in your precious name! The one who almost killed his wife while having a nightmare about the experience? My God, Sebastian. What's wrong with you?"

"Funny. I was about to ask you the same thing. You're blowing the thing with Twombley way out of proportion."

"Oh, hell." I rubbed my forehead. "I bet he'd love to hear that assessment. Dare I mention his wife? The woman who lost her first husband when our psychotic brother was trying to get even with you. Remember that? Or am I blowing that out of proportion too? A man died, Sebastian. I don't know how you even sleep at night, frankly."

I was actually winded after that diatribe, but my brother needed to hear every bit of it. The alarming part of it all was the way he stood and stared at me as though I was the one who was out of line.

When I was quiet for several minutes, he calmly said, "Are you done?"

His cavalier attitude infuriated me all over again.

"No, as a matter of fact, I'm not."

"Awesome," he muttered, but I heard the jerk.

The eye roll he paired with the childish remark sent me over the final edge.

"You're an asshole. Maybe everyone else outside your brainwashed posse is right. We haven't even covered that woman—shit, what was her name? The one who committed suicide supposedly but then became fish food in your swimming pool? How does Abbigail sleep in the same bed as you?" Then I just nodded. Like a wise old sage, I rubbed my chin and nodded in his direction.

"What?" he barked. At least he was showing some semblance of emotion now.

"She'll be next, dear brother. And understand this is not me wishing harm upon your house. This is me scared to death. For you, for your children, and for your wife. This cocky, *no one can touch me* attitude you're sporting is going to be your undoing."

Bas pinched the bridge of his nose and held the pose before speaking again. "Nothing will happen to anyone else. The whole mess is over now."

"How can you be sure?" I screeched, and my brother physically recoiled.

Okay, so my tone and volume had escalated into the nervous breakdown zone. I tried to take a few steadying breaths, but it was going to take longer than a minute and more than a few cleansing breaths to recover from this altercation.

"I'm scared, Sebastian. No. I'm terrified. For my family—for yours. For all of our friends. I don't know what it will take for you to see the writing on the wall."

"And what writing is that, Pia?"

"That your careless attitude and selfish actions are destroying everything good in your life. And the fact that I have to spell that out to you in such simple terms may be the most frightening part of all."

We were both furious now. Chests pumped in and out with angry breaths, bodies tensed in combative stances.

"What do you want from me? Seriously, what was the point of all this? I've bent over backward for you, Cassiopeia Shark, for our entire lives. Fuck me! If it weren't for me, you wouldn't even be alive. Maybe next time you come in here—into my fucking place of business—you could keep that little fact in the front of your entitled mind."

"How dare you," I gasped and staggered back a few steps as if he'd shoved me with his hands.

He knew he'd landed a critical hit. And living up to his reputation, he turned up the aggression while I was wounded.

"How dare I what? Speak the truth? Isn't that what we're doing here? Having some needless *Come to Jesus* moment?"

For the first time in the argument, I was speechless. After holding his dark, angry stare for a long moment, I recognized I was at my breaking point. So before he had to rescue me one more time—and no doubt add that to his tally sheet of people who owed him—I fled.

I snatched my coat and purse from the back of the sofa and strode toward the exit on very unsteady legs. There was no way I should be going anywhere until I calmed down and got my physical state under control, but I couldn't stay in this room for a moment longer.

Without a word of goodbye, I left my brother's plush office and didn't register another detail until the cool, fresh air of the street outside his building smacked me in the face.

Joel, his driver, was waiting at the curb and hustled to the rear passenger door when he saw me burst through the front doors.

"Afternoon, Ms. Shark."

I barely produced a smile for the man and instantly felt awful for it. That dumpster fire that just blazed up in the penthouse had nothing to do with this affable man.

"Hey, Joel," I greeted quietly.

"Calabasas?" he asked.

"Not today. Thank you, though. I have my car." I motioned with my chin in the direction of its parked location. "Just up the block."

He almost looked hesitant, and I wondered if Bas had called down to the loyal man and told him not to let me drive.

High-handed bastard.

"Have a good afternoon," I choked through the oncoming emotion. The moment I was in the safety of my own vehicle, a monumental meltdown was imminent. I couldn't remember the last time Bas and I fought like that. If ever.

EPILOGUE

Six months later...

An Interview with Los Angeles Businessman, Sebastian Shark
LA Street Scene
By A.C. Sandoval

Many think they know the infamous business mogul, Sebastian Shark. Recently, I sat down with the formidable man to discuss the latest irons he has in the fire. And trust me, there are plenty. What I didn't expect to uncover in our conversation was the deeply personal, emotional side of the enigmatic man the public rarely gets to see.

Shark is wearing a custom-tailored charcoal-gray suit, white button-down shirt, and a patterned, rust-colored tie. Small cobalt diamonds in the print pick up the striking color of the man's assessing gaze. We sat down in my cramped downtown office and had the following conversation.

ACS: Thank you for meeting with me today. And thank you for agreeing to the interview. I'm told you don't grant these one-on-one style meetings with the press very often, so I'm grateful.

Shark: Sure, no worries. [He smirks and hits me with a question of his own.] Are you saying someone had to tell you that? You didn't already know what a rare occasion this would be?

ACS: Yes and no. I know you aren't a fan of the mainstream media, but you've certainly had your share of time in the limelight.

Shark: Not by choice, of course.

ACS: Let me start by saying congratulations on the birth of your second child.

Shark: Thank you. Things are a little hectic at home right now with two children under two years. Sleep just doesn't happen like it used to. But my wife, Abbigail, and I are enjoying every minute of them both.

ACS: You've gone to great lengths to keep your children out of the media. Does that add to the stress?

Shark: Of course it does. We don't go out as often as we used to, so it can be a bit suffocating at home all the time.

ACS: Like many Angelinos, I'm excited to see your self-proclaimed "dream turned reality" building rising in the downtown skyline. Looks like you're nearing completion. Is there an opening day celebration scheduled?

Shark: I'm sure my PR team will put something together.

ACS: Is there a finish date in mind? From the looks of things at the jobsite, it should be wrapping up soon.

Shark: Yes, we're hoping by the end of next month. But, as I'm sure you can imagine, things don't always go as planned with projects of this magnitude. So that's a projection.

ACS: I'm glad you brought that up. Things going wrong during construction, I mean. You've definitely had your share of challenges on this project. Would you agree?

Shark: Any undertaking of this size is bound to have challenges. I'm just thrilled with the final outcome. That's where I try to focus.

ACS: Right. Makes sense. And you've overcome quite a

bit. In the infancy of the building, there was talk of the jobsite being cursed after a worker lost his life and your administrative assistant ended hers there. Do you know why she chose that particular location?

[Here, the man glares at me, not happy that I brought up the negative reminders.]

Shark: Sean Gibson losing his life was an unfortunate accident. Equipment malfunction—nothing more to it. That has been settled out of court with his widow, and we've all moved on.

ACS: His widow—Rio Gibson—is now married to your best friend and COO, Grant Twombley. Is that correct?

Shark: Yes, that's correct. And I'm happy to announce, with their permission, of course, that the Twombleys are expecting their first children next summer.

ACS: How wonderful! Did you say children?

Shark: Yes, Rio is currently carrying triplets.

ACS: The research done for this interview makes it seem like you have a very close-knit inner circle. Grant is married to Rio, who is also your wife's former sister-in-law and business partner, correct?

Shark: Yes, that's correct. And though my wife still mourns the loss of her brother every day, she is overjoyed for Grant and Rio. We all are.

ACS: And together the women own Abstract Catering, one of LA's most popular catering companies.

Shark: They did. Abbigail is no longer involved in that venture. She's concentrating on our two children at the moment.

ACS: And your sister, Cassiopeia Shark, is involved in your company as well?

Shark: No, she owns her own interior design firm, but the Edge is one of her main clients at the moment. I guess in that respect, we work together.

ACS: Did I read in the society news that she recently got engaged? To one of the Masterson boys to boot!

Shark: Yes, Jacob Masterson and my sister have a very long history. Everyone is very happy for them. No one deserves to be happy more than my sister.

ACS: What a lovely thing to say. Especially as a big brother who's been known to be very—shall we say—protective?

Shark: [laughs] Fair. That woman and I have been through a lot in our lives. More than most people know about or can imagine. I want nothing but the best of everything for her.

ACS: Since you brought up your past, can we talk a bit about that?

Shark: I guess it depends.

ACS: Okay, point taken. The world knows that you and your sister lost your mother when you were very young.

[Shark dips his chin in response.]

With Mother's Day coming in a few weeks, do you do anything special to honor her memory? How do you both handle her memory with your children?

[The pause before his answer is interminable. Fairly certain he wasn't going to answer, I was just about to ask another question when he shocked me with his heartfelt response.]

Shark: In the past few months, a lot of personal things have happened that have completely changed my outlook on life. Things that mattered before simply don't now. Our daughter's arrival had a lot to do with that. There's something about bringing a female into the world, for me, that made me look at life through different eyes. I also have the amazing privilege of being surrounded by very strong women. My wife and my sister in particular. My best friends' wives as well.

ACS: What's one thing specifically that's changed? That you view differently?

Shark: We need to treat each other, our fellow humans, with more kindness. Gentler, more lovingly, more compassionately. And don't get me wrong. I'm not insinuating women need to be handled with kid gloves. They're stronger than most men I know. Largely, the women in my life have shown me you don't have to be rough around the edges to be tough where it counts.

ACS: Are you worried about the future world for your daughter?

Shark: No. Not when we have the opportunity now to change things. The adults, the parents, the leaders of the world, I mean. We all have the chance to make changes now to make the future brighter for our children. We just have to take advantage of those openings. I, for one, vowed to start doing it myself. I hope others who look up to me as a role model will follow my example. We just have to use our own platforms to be the best we can be.

ACS: Those are very powerful words, Mr. Shark. I have to say, I'm very impressed and moved by your outlook. To be honest, it wasn't at all what I was expecting.

Shark: Well, like I've said, I'm making an effort to be a better human.

ACS: Thank you for sharing with me today. I feel honored that you trusted me with your opinions.

Shark: Of course. There are a few more exciting things I want to tell you about while we're doing all the feel-good stuff here. And again, this is all new to me, so I'm doing what I can with what I can control to make the world a better place. Starting right here with our very own city.

ACS: Oh, this already sounds exciting. Anything to make Los Angeles a better place—I'm here for it!

Shark: As I mentioned, I hope to finish construction on the Edge in the near future. Originally, the office space was going to be used as a revenue stream for my corporation in the form of leased and purchased commercial and residential parcels. We've retooled our financial model and will be taking applications from nonprofit organizations first. Those office spaces will be under lease, as originally planned, but they will be rent free, or very low rent if a tax break from paying rent is available that benefits the tenant.

ACS: Wow, that's really a drastic change. When and where will nonprofits be able to apply for these leases? And how will you choose who gets the space if you have more applicants than units?

Shark: I'm glad you asked both those questions. We are currently accepting applications online only, and that application can be found at theedge.com/lease. I've assembled a team to review the applications and investigate the legitimacy of the organizations. From there, they will have the very unenviable task of choosing the nonprofits that get to take advantage of this incredible opportunity.

ACS: Mr. Shark—

Shark: Oh, one other thing. I forgot to mention these will be five-year leases to start. But most charities I'm involved with personally would welcome five years rent-free. Especially with rent being so astronomical in this city.

ACS: Oh, agreed. This is a very generous venture you're spearheading.

Shark: Again, it's about leading by example. Each of us taking the opportunities we have access to, to make the world a better place. Kindness inspiring kindness.

ACS: Well, I can't thank you enough for announcing such exciting news here with me today. And thank you for taking the time out of your busy schedule to sit down with me. I wish you all the best with your business, your family, and whatever else you take on. I think the world hasn't seen the last of Sebastian Shark.

Continue Reading for a preview of the first book in the Shark's Edge spin-off:

Brentwood Bombshells

CHAPTER ONE

AGATHA

Bright. *Too* bright. So bright, even with my lids still closed, the obnoxious light beams were making my head throb worse.

Oh my God, my head.

This had to be the literal worst part of excessive drinking. The morning after was brutal, and this one was no different than the times I'd done this to myself before.

Cautiously, I patted the mattress beside me.

Shit.

There was definitely another person in bed with me. Luckily, when I listened a bit longer, whoever it was continued sleeping. The soft sounds of air moving in and out through parted lips made panic rise. Was that a chic?

Not again.

I had no idea what *that* was about lately, but on more than one occasion, I took a woman home with me. It had never been my thing before, but to be honest, I'd been pretty fed up with the male population.

We couldn't all be as lucky as my oldest sister, Hannah. The incredibly fine specimen she had sunk her teeth into could right the wrongs for so many douchebags before him. If I could just sit and stare at that guy, it would be suitable penance for all of mankind.

Infinitesimally, I turned my head, not wanting to wake my bedmate and deal with the awkward morning-after conversation. At the same time, curiosity killed this cat every single time. I needed to know who I so carelessly shared my body with the night before.

Although...after a quick assessment of things beneath the blankets, I was fully clothed. And ewww, I needed a shower in the worst way. There was my out—I just had to be stealthy when exiting the bed.

But first, I had to figure out where the hell I was.

Parts of the room seemed familiar, or at least what I could see from my current vantage point. I slid my hand across the mattress to estimate how close I was to the edge. If I could slither off the bed without creating much motion, I could get to the shower to freshen up. Nothing worse than having the morning-after conversation with a stranger when your mouth tasted like you may have barfed a time or two.

So, fine, this was not my proudest moment. And also fine, this kind of bullshit was happening a little too often lately. I needed to stage an intervention with myself and stop this shit before I did something really stupid.

I made it to the bathroom without waking my party pal. At least there was some relief when I saw it was a guy and he was someone I knew. Probably explained why my clothes were still on. Carmen Sandoval was a strait-laced mama's boy who would never take advantage of a drunk woman.

Even if she were—

Wait. What the fuck am I wearing?

My stomach roiled as I gaped at my reflection. Whether the letters were backward or not, even an idiot could read what my T-shirt said.

BRIDE

No. Please no.

I instantly dropped my eyes to the cheap green jelly band on my left finger. Well, at least drunk me got the color right. Green was my favorite...

I was desperate to find bright spots in what was looking like a monumental disaster. Trying to calm down, I stripped off the offensive shirt and angrily threw it into the neighboring sink. It had to be a joke.

This is a joke, right?

I tugged off my leggings and panties and left them in a heap on the floor. The massive showers in these villas were glorious, and this one was calling to me like a siren.

Under the spray, I tried in vain to recall the events of the night before. My sister and one of her bosses, Rio Gibson, married the men of their dreams, shotgun style, at a cheesy little chapel on the strip. Afterward, we had a fantastic meal in one of our hotel's restaurants and played many hands of poker until everyone was shitfaced or exhausted.

Guess which one I was?

I remembered doing a lot of shots in that card room, and things went really fuzzy from that point of the night onward. I leaned my head back farther to rinse the suds from my long hair and racked my brain a bit more.

Did I leave the property? I must have at some point, because this she-she hotel didn't sell tacky souvenirs like the one I woke up wearing. Maybe it was Hannah's and I borrowed it after a spill or vomit episode. That sounded pretty reasonable, so I held on to the concept with all the functioning parts of my brain and stepped out of the marble enclosure to dry off.

I startled when the door pushed open and a sleepy Carmen staggered in. One eye still closed, he rubbed at the other one. His hair was rioting in every possible direction from a hard sleep, and the erection tenting his boxers couldn't be missed.

"Morning," he mumbled as he shuffled past me to go to the separate toilet section of the villa's expansive bathroom. He closed the door behind him, and in a few beats, I could hear him relieving himself. The occupants in the neighboring villa might have heard him as well, because the sound was incredibly loud.

Is that a man in there or a horse?

I chuckled at my nonsense and leaned in closer to the mirror to survey the damage.

Normally I would expect bloodshot eyes and super dry skin, but this morning I actually had several bruises on my face, neck, and what I could see of my body peeking out from the towel.

Was there a brawl?

Wouldn't be the first time for that, either.

While I quickly searched around the bathroom for the luxurious white robe the hotel provided, Carmen shuffled to the sink to wash his hands. Even after peeing, his dick stood at attention.

When he cleared his throat, I realized I had stopped mid-tie of the robe's belt to stare at his physique. Not going to lie, the man looked good...until I noticed his shirt.

GROOM

I shot my eyes to his left hand, and sure enough, green jelly band on his ring finger too.

I popped my eyes up to find him staring at me via the mirror and my shoulders dropped low.

"What did we do?" I croaked in the most pathetic voice, rubbing my throbbing forehead in distress.

"Got irresponsibly drunk, for starters," he answered cautiously.

"And?" My voice pitched higher by the slightest bit, but my volume shot considerably louder than it had been.

He recoiled from the decibels and answered sheepishly. "Looks like we caught the wedding fever that's been going around."

ALSO BY VICTORIA BLUE

Shark's Edge Series:
(with Angel Payne)
Shark's Edge
Shark's Pride
Shark's Rise
Grant's Heat
Grant's Flame
Grant's Blaze

★

Elijah's Whim
Elijah's Want
Elijah's Need
Jacob's Star
Jacob's Eclipse

Misadventures:
Misadventures with a Book Boyfriend
Misadventures at City Hall

Secrets of Stone Series:
(with Angel Payne)
No Prince Charming
No More Masquerade
No Perfect Princess
No Magic Moment
No Lucky Number
No Simple Sacrifice
No Broken Bond
No White Knight
No Longer Lost

For a full list of Victoria's other titles,
visit her at VictoriaBlue.com

ABOUT VICTORIA BLUE

International bestselling author Victoria Blue lives in her own portion of the galaxy known as Southern California. There, she finds the love and life-sustaining power of one amazing sun, two unique and awe-inspiring planets, and four indifferent yet comforting moons. Life is fantastic and challenging and every day brings new adventures to be discovered. She looks forward to seeing what's next!

Visit her at VictoriaBlue.com

ACKNOWLEDGMENTS

Thank you to the team at Waterhouse Press for supporting this series to the very last page. It has been a professional honor writing under your name. Thank you, Scott Saunders, for every moment you devoted to these characters, stories, and series as a whole. As always, your guidance and expertise made each word shine.

Personal gratitude for Megan Ashley, Amy Bourne, and Faith Moreno for keeping my social media life active and interesting. Also, for the love and support and daily cheerleading you each provide. In your own way, you each make me a better writer and a better human.

And a very special thank you to Angel Payne. We came up with this idea as a team, and I'm honored and grateful you trusted me to see the story through to the end on my own. I hope I did the characters and stories justice in your very talented eyes.